THE
LAST VOYAGE
OF CAPTAIN
REDFEARN

LAIR
4

D.V. SULLIVAN

TRANSMARINIA PRESS

ISBN ebook: 979-8-9866781-8-4
ISBN paperback: 978-1-966623-99-1

For readers 18+. Contains brief descriptions of domestic violence.

Transmarinia Press
2709 N Hayden Island Dr
STE 330550
Portland, OR 97217

You deserve love

ONE

CAPTAIN REDFEARN

Back in the day, those old sea tars always had a patron saint. You know, some heavenly advocate believed to grant protection and good luck.

I'm starting to think she's mine.

Call it coincidental, but she always happens to be on the aft main deck when I return. Her white yachtie shirt flashes like a beacon, as perfectly smooth and blinding as the hull of my *Lair*. She has her hands clasped before her, her hooded eyes imperious, her tight bun of silky Asian hair as polished as anchor housing in the sunshine of Monaco. Something inside me eases at the sight of her, and I can't help but grin.

Damn, she's a beautiful woman.

"Well?" she calls as the tender floats up to the superyacht's swim deck.

I wipe my face smooth and hop out, let the deckhands take over berthing the tender. "You were right as always," I admit with a grunt, and make for the stairs leading up to the main deck. I have to force myself not to bound up them like a giddy schoolboy. "Mr. Voper went for it. Didn't even hesitate when he saw her picture. We've officially hired our fourth stew."

Mrs. Colding nods, her lips creasing in the slightest suggestion of satisfaction. I don't mind that she's distracted. I'm too busy breathing in through my nose to savor what I've been waiting for the entire trip back—that scent with its hints of sandalwood and Asian blossoms, delicate and sophisticated.

I have to stop myself from closing my eyes.

"We should have bet on it," she muses.

I take my time responding. I'm enjoying the thought of undoing that fucking bun of hers so I can run my rough hands through her hair.

"You know I don't bet," I say when I'm ready. "Not anymore."

She turns to me, her fine lashes lifting to show deep brown eyes solemn with sympathy. "I know."

I know she does; nothing escapes her attention. She files everything away—every fact, every preference, every quirk of someone's personality—as a chief stew needs to know everything to deliver perfect service. But it's more than that—she cares more about the needs of others than her own. Because she's loyal. Over the years, I've done my own filing away of facts: the storing up of every detail I can get on Mrs. Colding. How she dismisses coffee as a crutch for weaklings, but has a weakness for Coca-Cola when she needs a boost. How fingerprints on reflective surfaces make her skin crawl. How she probably struggles with a major case of OCD, which I find adorable. But most of all, I love that her icy exterior hides the biggest, warmest heart I have ever known.

She's still looking at me. Those eyes curve in what could almost be mistaken for humor. "But a more devious woman would have taken advantage of the opportunity."

I love it when she teases me. It's often so subtle, most men wouldn't pick up on it. It's taken *me* years to pick up on it. But that's what I admire about her. Her subtlety. Her class.

At least, I *hope* she was teasing me.

Because I'd know what that would mean.

I've had my doubts, for sure. Working with someone for this long without knowing if your feelings are reciprocated, it's hard not to. But I didn't want to spoil it. It was enough to just be around her. To be in her presence. That was what living taught you. That sometimes not risking a thing is better. Better to keep it alive as a sweet drip of hurt, safe and dependable. A love that knows its place. These are the things that, though they never risk the trials of high romance, sustain you through the dark patches of life.

No. I didn't want to ruin that.

But what if there could be more?

"You think it'll work?" I ask, pushing away my thoughts.

"The plan? To shake that old grump out of his grief?" She turns to study the tinted glass doors of the *Lair*. "I think everyone deserves a second chance."

I lift a brow. "Everyone?"

She frowns at me. "Are you inferring something, Captain Redfearn?"

I shrug. "I'm inferring you deserve it too, even though you never consider it."

The frown deepens. "You've lost me."

Christ, I hope not.

This is ridiculous. I've been in the Navy. I've dealt with Adrian's kind. I've crawled my way out of the darkest places a man can fall into. And somehow saying what I'm about to say to this woman makes me more terrified than I've ever been in my life.

I square my shoulders and face her.

"We've known each other for some time now."

She faces me, that quizzical furrow still between her brows. "We have."

"I'd like to think we know each other well."

She is very, very still. "We do."

"And I don't, I mean . . ." My hands are shaking, and I wipe one rough palm against the other to try to still them.

She watches all this, alarmed. "Redfearn? What is it?"

Just get it out already.

"We've both been through enough to know what we want. And I know because of your past you've had no interest in . . . and Lord knows I've had my own reasons for not . . ."

She blinks at me, waiting.

"I mean to say, maybe both of us thought we were done with romance. But I've lived enough to recognize something special when I see it. And I've never met a more incredible woman than you." I let out a big, wavering breath. I can't look at her. I know if I do, if I see how she's responding to this, I might stop. "So if you think you'd ever be open to that, just let me know. There's no rush. I—I'll wait for you."

And I do. I've never heard a more awful silence. All I can hear is the raucous screech of gulls, my own unsteady breathing.

When I can't stand it any longer, I look at her.

I've never seen that expression on her face before. I have no reference for it. She looks as if she's been winded, as if she's just witnessed some terrible accident. Her shoulders rise and fall. She presses a hand to her stomach and lets out a shivery breath between her lips, looks at me and shakes her head. "Captain Redfearn," she whispers.

My heart drops.

"*Fuck*," I hiss, running a hand through my hair. "I'm sorry, I shouldn't have said anything—"

"No!" she says hastily. "I don't mind that you said that—"

"Yeah," I grunt, rolling my eyes and turning away. *Great, she didn't mind.* "Yeah, all right—"

"No," she says again, and I look down to find she's gripping my arm. A shy, disbelieving smile plays about her lips. "I meant, I *really* didn't mind."

I feel my soul fall back into my body. "Oh. You—you didn't?"

She shakes her head, lips curved.

The blood drains from my brain. I feel light-headed, breathless, struck silly. A goofy grin splashes across my face.

I'm not the only one.

"Actually," she says, and heat pinks her pale skin. "I think there's a part of me that's been waiting for you to say that ever since . . ."

But I don't hear the rest of her words. Because blood is booming in my ears like the beat of doom. Because the impossible is happening. Something has unfolded itself from the deckhead above Mrs. Colding in eerie silence: Evangeline Voper, in a lacy choir girl's dress. Hanging upside down like some batlike creature so she can craft her fangs into Mrs. Colding's neck in a heavy unrivering of blood.

All the air leaves my lungs.

"Redfearn," Mrs. Colding chokes, her eyes wide.

And my howl of anguish fills the world.

I jerk awake with my heart wanting to pound out of my chest and look about. Rain lashes the porthole. Lightning flares, illuminating a dark, industrial-looking cabin in stark white flashes. For a panic-stricken moment, I don't remember where or when I am, have to claw my way out of that dream and remind myself that it's okay. Mrs. Colding is alive. That bloodsucking bitch didn't kill her. She asked me to give her time.

The ship groans like a dying whale, pipes clanking. Definitely not the *Lair*. Definitely not a superyacht. When I glance at the cot opposite mine, a face jumps out at me in one of those bursts of white—my bunkmate eyeing me warily, one arm folded under his head, his body as wiry and tatted as a convict's. And I remember what vessel I'm on.

I'd somehow fallen asleep in the storm.

I sigh and slide a hand down my face in a rasping of stubble, try to steady my heartrate as the power of that dream fades away. Then I reach under my pillow to make sure it's still there.

My captain's log, its faded brown leather smooth under my fingers.

There's no chance I'll fall asleep again. Not after that dream. Not now that I'm thinking about why I'm here, what I have to do.

Time for another entry.

CAPTAIN'S LOG

Transmarinia to Fort Lauderdale, December 5th.
Ship: *Isolato*.
Speed: 18 knots.
Distance: 4,732 mi.
Weather: Stormy, rough seas.
Notes: Can't seem to shake habit of log keeping. Don't even have my own ship at present. Suppose this has turned into confession of sorts.

I suppose I'm speaking to you.

I've taken passage aboard an old rusting freighter. Should take a week for crossing to the States. Don't mind added time or rough weather. Safer this way. Nosferyachtu Club may be looking for me, after all. Need to think like a fugitive. Paid captain to ensure I'm not on books. Can't say I trust bunkmate either—looks like he'd knife me in my sleep. Can handle men like that though. Only thing I don't care for is spare time for thinking. Damn if it wasn't hard to leave Arie. Can't think about it without my chest aching. But she doesn't need me anymore. And other people do.

Now to rally myself for what's ahead. First, checking in on Mrs. Colding. Making sure she's okay. Don't know how I'll feel seeing her again. Will be even harder to leave her.

But I have to. Because I need to find you. I need to find my missing daughter.

I love you, Penelope. Remember what I'd say? When I'd tuck you in as a little girl?

You're my little sun.

TWO
MRS. COLDING

When they release me from the hospital, I ask to be taken straight to Colding Mansion.

The state of my Uber is appalling. There's lint and hairs on the back seat, gum wrappers and empty water bottles on the floor. And the windows are a horror—they're smudged everywhere in fingerprints and look like they've never seen soap or a chamois. These windows will be in my nightmares. I sit perched on the edge of the back seat, spine stiff and hands curled into themselves on my bare knees, using every last ounce of my will to not break down and launch into a frenzy of cleaning. To distract myself, I look out the window and watch Fort Lauderdale's multimillion-dollar waterfront properties glide past.

I'd forgotten what it would be like on land. No standards. No pride. Dirt everywhere and getting everywhere. Gone is my perfect *Lair*. Gone is my spick-and-span boat, my stews to direct, my owner whose consuming needs had saved me with their day-to-day challenges from ever facing the terrible duty of figuring out who I was.

In short, gone is my purpose in life.

I'm a bloody landlubber again.

I spy the shapes of yachts glinting in the sun along the canals and an immense yearning narrows my throat. It's happening again. That on-and-off weight on my chest that makes it hard to breathe, that anxiety that's been creeping in ever since I got back on land. I force it down.

My driver is watching me in the rearview again.

He's young. He must be, as he still doesn't know how to iron a shirt. (I'd never let any of my stews get away with those wrinkles.) He hasn't yet learned the art of subtlety either. He keeps stealing glances at me, has been since he picked me up at the hospital. I know what he's looking at.

The stitches.

It's understandable. There were a lot more of them than I thought there'd be.

I don't mind him staring—I long ago decided I wouldn't let any man make me feel embarrassed about how I look. That doesn't mean it's not rude though.

I roll my eyes to the rearview and lift a brow, and the driver flushes.

"Dog bite?" he ventures sheepishly.

I turn to the window and watch my reflection smirk back at me. "Well," I drawl, thinking of Evangeline Voper. "It was a bitch all right."

It's hard not to think about that without thinking about how I left the *Lair*. The dazzling, heartbreaking sweetness of Adrian Voper loving me too much to put me in harm's way anymore, and the humiliation of being let go. But deeper than that, a feeling of bereavement and helplessness. I can't even help from afar. Adrian had warned me that I shouldn't check in on him and Arie, because I'd only get worried. He knows me too well.

And then there's Captain Redfearn.

An unbearable tenderness squeezes my heart at the thought of him. I don't want to trust in that, as much as I trust him. As much as I trust what he promised me. *(I'll see you soon.)* What he's helping Arie do is too dangerous for me to place any hope in his return. I've trained myself over many years, after all, to not place my trust in hope.

I am on my own.

The Uber slows to a stop and I look up to find we've arrived at Colding Mansion.

The sight of it makes my heart clench in my chest. It's lost none of its grandness in the intervening years, a hulk of Mediterranean Revival architecture with a rose stucco façade. But that rosy plaster has now been stained by dirt and time. Withered bougainvilleas cling in dry webs of vines to its turrets and wrought-iron balconies, and its terracotta roof is either missing tiles or is engulfed in patches of some kind of creeping rot. Palm trees droop about it, unkempt and diseased-looking, and those monstrously huge azaleas with their pink and purple blooms have succumbed to root rot and encroached on the driveway. Even the wrought-iron gates have been choked by some kind of dying vine, giving it all the effect of some half-hidden gothic Xanadu. When I'd first seen this place, I'd thought it had an air of the fairy tale about it. I thought I'd been rescued.

How naïve I'd been.

"You sure this is the right place?" the Uber driver asks in a dubious whisper.

"Yes," I say as I stare up at that ghost from the past, my lips forming a grim line. "I'm sure."

I wait for the Uber to leave before I take out the old remote for the gates and click.

With a rattling shriek of metal, the gates come to life, sweep inward in a rustling and unraveling of vines.

Carefully smoothing my hair back, I walk through the gates and approach the front door.

The world suddenly seems very loud. The razzing of insects coming from the rotting garden flowers. My heels clicking on the cracked and overgrown pavement of the sweeping drive. My heart pushing its way up into my throat. With every step, I think of my younger self, that self who should have turned back, who I could not warn. Who walked, as I am walking now, into the lair of what had the power to destroy me.

Sweat collects along my spine, under my arms. I lift my chin.

I am not afraid. He's gone now. He holds no power over me.

The key I've kept all these years is shaking as it scrapes into the lock. Still fits.

The door groans when I open it.

The sound echoes into a stale darkness. It's as vast as I remember it: The grand hall with its cold marble and Chinese antiquities. The high, arched windows with their towering red curtains blocking out the light. The sweeping staircase with its wrought-iron banister, the upstairs gallery with its maze of empty rooms. The emptiness—that was the same. The lack of furniture, of warmth, of life. Cold. But with a veil of dust and disuse on everything now. This stillness of neglect and the shadow of trauma. This seal.

I blink, my eyes adjusting to the darkness, and every stewardess instinct in me recoils.

I'd thought that Uber had been bad. That veil is more than just dust—it is patches of mold mottling the marble tiles of the floor, cobwebs spanning the corners, rat droppings like black rice everywhere. Decades of disuse built up in a pungent reek of decay, lingering like the foul residue of the mansion's owner.

I stand there in the hall, hand to stomach, ready to run, an irrational terror tightening my throat. I know he's dead. I know he's gone. And still. I can feel him. I can feel his presence here, as if he still lurked in these shadows, as if he had been waiting for me, all these years, to come back to him. To tell me that I belong here with him.

Not out of character for him, not out of character at all, if he were to come up behind me now and—

"There you are, my little empress."

The hairs on my arms stand straight up. I whirl about, my heart hammering in my breast, a scream wanting to get out. I have to scream. It can't be—

Nothing. No shadow amongst the marble halls. No Mr. Colding.

Still gone.

Just me. Me, and the fear he's left me with. The fear I thought I'd left behind.

My teeth grind together. My hands ball at my sides. The blood boils in my veins, making everything turn red with fury.

All right, then.

The cleaning supplies are where I remember them. Downstairs hall, by the back door. Mop. Bucket. Water. Soap. These things are eternal. Cleanliness is divine.

Time to do what I know best. Time to rid myself of him once and for all.

I start upstairs and work my way down, as on a yacht. Dusting the crown molding free of cobwebs, shaking out the window curtains, stripping off the white furniture sheets with their layers of filth. Then on to vacuuming and mopping. The stairs. The grand hall. I'm on all fours in gloves and a breathing mask scrubbing out mold with bleach when I break down, shivering, my hands braced on the marble floor, the backs of my eyes scalded with unshed tears.

How has he taken everything from me? I thought I'd remade my life, moved beyond him. And here I am, back where I started, back where it all began, stripped of purpose.

I'm nothing without my role on the *Lair*. I'm nothing on land.

I'm nothing.

It takes me a week to clean the house. My neck is stiff and throbbing by the time I lug the last of the trash out the door. I throw the tall curtains back to let in the sun and take in the vast arches of marble with both exhaustion and a sense of accomplishment, of having cleansed a great darkness.

You're gone now. I'm better than you. I got *the better of you.*

Then the skin at the back of my neck crawls.

I can feel it watching me. I've been avoiding it ever since I got back. I haven't looked at it once.

I turn about to stare out the windows.

It's still there. His 30-foot Sunseeker Predator yacht suspended in the shiplift at the edge of the canal, stained with rust, its sheeted topside covered in dead palm leaves. Where it all ended.

Where it still hasn't ended.

Because I can see it. It must be a trick of the light, the sun glaring down through the palms in a blinding haze of gold. But for a moment I see blood splashed on its hull and white sheet. Two bodies on the dock. Mr. Colding and my old love, Miguel . . .

I twitch the curtains shut and stand there staring at the rich fabric, breathing hard. No amount of cleaning can exorcise that memory. That needs to go.

I turn back into the cold, immaculate darkness of the mansion to grab my phone. Time to make a call. Have a boat salvage company tow that wreck away.

Beyond that, I don't know what's to come of me. I don't know what to do with my life. It's a terrifying blank.

Maybe—

I stop when I see the shadow framed in the front doorway. My heart jumps into my throat. My skin sings. I shake my head.

No. No, I banished you—

"Mrs. Colding?"

And the shadow steps into the light, turning into Captain Arnold Redfearn.

My stomach freefalls. My jaw hangs. I want to sob laughter. I want to laugh sobs.

It's him. Unmistakably him. Tall, broad-shouldered, still fit for a man in his fifties, and with that swoop of sterling-gray hair. Dashing, one could say. His white yachtie polo and khaki shorts are rumpled from travel, and there's a silver glint of stubble to his jaw.

Him.

He jerks a thumb. "I knocked but there was no—are you okay?"

My answer is running into the solid, dependable weight of him, almost knocking him over, my arms flying around his neck. I can't squeeze hard enough. *I'm safe*, is all I can think. *I've been saved.*

There's a grin in his voice. "Hello to you too."

Heat floods my cheeks. I step back, smoothing my bun back into place, hoping he can't see me blushing. "I didn't expect you so soon," I say, quite calmly, not quite looking at him.

He suppresses a grin for my benefit. "Yes. It was sooner than I thought too. Arie didn't need me anymore."

My heart thuds again. "Is she—"

"Fine. They're both fine. She's . . . decided to take Volok out herself."

I can't help but smile. "Sounds like Arie."

The captain grins, caught between admiration and wonder. "Yeah. But if anyone can do it . . ."

I nod, and a silence falls between us.

I don't know what to do—which does not happen often. I'm all fluttery with nerves. I must look ridiculous. *This* is ridiculous. I have always prided myself on my composure. How can this man have this effect on me?

He tips his head and studies me with those piercingly clear gray eyes. "How is . . .?"

I instinctively flutter a hand to my neck before dropping it. "Not bad. The stitches have come out . . ."

He's already closed the space between us, and I turn my head to accommodate him. His face slackens when he sees the ugly snaggle of raw, pink skin, the two puncture marks that will soon turn to silvery scars. A hard, protective anger surfaces in his eyes, edged with a tenderness that makes me hold my breath. He lifts a hand callused by countless boat washdowns and gently, very gently, touches my skin.

"Does it hurt?" he asks, his voice hard, but not unkind.

"No," I say, barely saying it, barely breathing.

We're very close.

Redfearn seems to realize this. He swallows, turns his head slightly to look into my eyes, and I feel a thrilling twist in my stomach. When his eyes drop to my lips, I know what he's thinking. I'm thinking of it, too. That kiss. That kiss he'd given me before I was medevacked off the *Lair*. The memory of it hangs between us, thrumming with tension, posing the question: *Am I ready?*

He takes a step back.

My skin is still buzzing, warm and tingling, where he touched me.

"Well," he says, clearing his throat, and tries for a more formal tone. "I'm glad you're doing well."

My heart sinks.

"I wanted to check in on you, before—you remember that I'm—"

"Going to find your daughter."

He nods. Then looks at me. It's been a long time, a very long time, since a man has looked at me like that.

I don't know if any man has ever looked at me that way.

His throat bobs. "I just wanted to see you again, before—"

A cool, collected firmness takes hold of me, making me feel like myself again. "Let me stop you right there," I say, lifting a hand. "There's no way I'm not going with you."

His face falls. "I can't ask you to—"

"Yes, you can." I glance around at the palatial emptiness of Colding Mansion. "There's no way I'm staying here. I'm not going to twiddle my thumbs while you go off on your own to find your daughter." I give him a look that's somewhere between glaring and pleading, my voice low. "Please don't leave me here."

He opens his mouth, shuts it. He's never seen this side of me. He's never seen me ask for anything.

He's already given in.

I draw myself up. "So. Now that's taken care of," I conclude in a bright, crisp tone, mentally dusting my hands, and arch a brow with the faintest trace of a smile. "Where do we start?"

THREE
CAPTAIN REDFEARN

I pace the gas station parking lot while I wait for the call to go through.

The gas station is typical of Florida: a white-painted icebox pumping out A/C into the sweltering heat, its palmetto-fringed parking lot splotched with iridescent oil stains. Heat wafts up from the pavement, and already drops of sweat are gliding down my spine, sticking my shirt to my back. I'm not looking forward to this conversation.

I glance over at Mrs. Colding waiting by the rental car. She's trying not to look my way, and though outwardly composed as ever, I can tell she feels awkward.

Of course she'd be, knowing who I'm calling.

"Hello?" The sound of Margaret's voice on the phone sets my heart pounding in my chest.

I turn away.

"Hey," I say. "It's me."

There's a long silence.

"I thought of texting, but—I didn't think you'd respond."

"You're probably right." Her voice is low, worn out, wary. "New number, huh?"

"Yeah," I say, unsure of how to navigate this conversation. "New a lot of things."

Margaret lets out a dry bark of laughter. "You'll have to pardon me if that's hard to believe."

I look down at my shoes. "I stopped drinking, Marg. Gambling, too."

Another silence.

"I know I . . . didn't handle it well. Somehow, I was stupid enough to think that turning to all that stuff would—" I falter, feeling her anger and silent accusation radiating out of the phone like the heat all around me. It makes me wilt. "I know we weren't married anymore, but . . ." My chest tightens, an ache moving up into my throat. "I should have been there. I shouldn't have left you to face that alone."

No response. For a moment I think she's hung up.

"I'm sorry," I go on, my voice beginning to break, the words I've wanted to say for years spilling out. "I never said I'm sorry and I—"

"Don't." The word is like a hand help up, as if she can't risk a crack in the dam she's erected inside herself to hold back a terrifying deluge of grief. "Please, just—" She sighs, sounding like she has her head in her hands. "Why are you calling, Arnold?"

I square my shoulders and pull myself together. I can feel Mrs. Colding's eyes on the back of my neck, my ears turning red.

I clear my throat and say, "I'm going to find her."

There's a brittle, crackling squeak, as if Margaret has sunk down into a wicker-bottomed chair. I can feel her mind working this over. "Penelope?"

"I want to make amends. I want to find her and make things right."

The frail hope in her voice narrows my throat. "You think you can?"

I nod, feeling my jaws grind together. "I'll do everything in my power."

Her voice changes now, becomes practical. "What do you need from me?"

"An address. Her best friend's. Melody, I think it was—"

"I have it." She draws in a steadying breath. "I don't know if this will make up for what you did. But if you can—if you do this—"

"I can," I growl, straightening my spine. "I will."

I can feel her own nod through the phone. "Bring our baby back, Arnold."

I knock on the door of the flamingo-pink condo and wait.

The beachfront complex in Fort Lauderdale is picture perfect: preternaturally green lawns, waving palm trees. It doesn't quiet any of my anxiety.

"Penelope moved in with her best friend before she disappeared," I explain. "If anyone would know where she'd be . . ."

Mrs. Colding nods, not quite meeting my eyes. I can tell she still feels a little self-conscious after my phone call with my ex-wife. So do I, for that matter. I can't help but worry she thinks there's something still there. I consider explaining things, and restrain myself. She knows. She must know.

How can she not know how I feel about her?

Seeing her again is like the heady, breathless rush you get from winning the jackpot at the casino: the same addictive overwhelming of the senses. It had almost knocked me over before she'd even run into my arms and filled my nose with that intoxicating scent of hers. I'm still dizzy from it. Dizzy from the cascade of memory. Dizzy from her jolting beauty that never fails to surprise me. When I'd come across her in Colding Mansion, she must have been cleaning. *Of course* she'd been cleaning. Everything had smelled of the chemical tang of bleach and she glistened in a fine sheen of sweat, flyaway hairs escaping from her bun to dangle in soft black wisps about her face. A few of them still do. It takes everything I have to not tuck them behind her ear.

The condo's front door opens and I glimpse a young woman, nose ring glinting, peeling a blood orange. Red citrus mists the air. "Yeah?"

"Hello, Melody? I'm Mr. Redfearn. Pen's father."

The woman's tone changes. "Oh. Hey."

I glance at Mrs. Colding, a bad feeling stirring in my gut. "I, uh, was wondering . . . do you happen to know where

Penelope is? I haven't been able to get in touch with her for a while."

Melody slouches haughtily in the doorframe to scrutinize me. She's wearing short-shorts and a bikini top, nothing else. She bites into the blood orange and gory pulp bathes her chin, drips red and wet about her bare feet. I swallow and glance over at Mrs. Colding. She's wincing, and a hand has flown unconsciously to the raw skin at her neck. So. She was traumatized by that event, too.

It's a long time before Melody responds. "I don't know if she'd want me to tell you, Mr. Redfearn."

I look down at my deck shoes, a sudden tightness in my throat.

Farther inside the flamboyantly-colored condo, there's a male rumble. "Who is it?"

Melody wrenches her head around and shouts back, "Pen's dad. You know, the drunk?"

I flinch, the blood mounting in my cheeks. I can feel Mrs. Colding watching me with sad, sympathetic eyes.

I shift my weight.

"I'm sorry to bother you. I just . . . I'm worried about her. And I want to make amends." I clamp my jaw and try to steady myself. "Please."

There's a long, conflicted pause.

Then Melody arms the citrus from her chin.

"I'm only telling you this because I'm worried, too." She sighs, flicking a seed out of her orange. "I haven't heard from her in a year now."

My pulse quickens. It's hard not to pace. "A year? Have you called the non-profit she volunteered at—"

"She didn't volunteer at a non-profit, Mr. Redfearn." Melody's voice is too drained of feeling to even bother with accusation. All that's left is disgust. "She went into the yachting industry. To find *you*."

I freeze. "To find—" I shake my head. It doesn't make sense. "Why didn't she just—"

"I don't know." Melody blows out a breath. "I think she wanted to prove something." She widens her eyes as she studies her orange, tilting her head back and forth. "That she was worthy of your love or whatever."

I close my lids. "Jesus."

Mrs. Colding drifts closer. She raises a hand and, very hesitantly, touches my arm. "Do you have any idea where she might be?" she asks Melody. "Anything that could help us?"

Melody eyes Mrs. Colding up and down, shakes her head. "Sorry. Can't help you." She makes to shut the door.

"Wait!" I brace a palm on the wood. "Please—"

Melody pokes her head out, teeth clenched. "She hated you, you know that?" she spits, the sudden anger like a slap. "This is what happens when you abandon your daughter."

Everything in me shrinks away from the words. I blink. My stomach tightens. My throat grows tight. "I know. I'm just trying to make it up to her."

"Kinda too late for that now, don't you think?" She lifts her hand like the claw in a toy machine, eyes locked on mine, and lets her orange splat at my feet. Blood-colored fruit flesh splatters my deck shoes.

She slams the door.

I stand there feeling like a mule has kicked me in the chest. It's hard to breathe. There's a prickling behind my eyes.

Mrs. Colding watches me. She very gently grips my arm, tugs me around. "Come on. We'll find a way. We know she's in the yachting industry now. It'll—it'll take some time to track her down, but we can—"

"Mr. Redfearn."

We turn. Melody stands in the doorway, stiff with a sort of wary nonchalance, a guilty offering of goodwill. "Pen left a box of her stuff here." She shrugs a shoulder. "If you wanna look at it."

The condo feels like the tropics. The flamingo pink continues inside, mingling with floral wallpaper and a linoleum floor. A fan rattles humid air over us as Melody drops a cardboard box onto a table in the living room. "Have at it," she says and plops onto the couch beside a Cuban guy in Bermuda shorts and a striped guayabera, a ginormous bong held to his lips. "You take all of it again?" she grumbles.

I look down at the box. At PENELOPE scrawled in black marker on its top. I glance at Mrs. Colding.

I unfold the cardboard flaps as if expecting a bomb to go off.

The first thing I see are the postcards, dozens of them with vintage illustrations of far-flung destinations: THE MALDIVES, SARDINIA, KARPATHOS. On their backs my crude chicken scratches: "Daddy's thinking of you," "I miss you," "I love you," "I wish you'd write to me," "You're my little sun."

Heat scorches the backs of my eyes. My heart swells. Everything blurs up and becomes far away.

She kept them. She'd kept all of them.

Mrs. Colding puts her hand on mine.

Then she reaches into the box and comes up with a handful of business cards: CREW FINDERS, LUXURY YACHT GROUP, ELITE CREW INTERNATIONAL.

"She was looking at crew agencies," she says and turns to the couch. "Do you know if a crew agency got her staffed?"

"No idea," Melody sighs, sparking a cigarette lighter and lighting the bong.

"Wait," says her boyfriend, rousing from his daze with pothead dignity. "Wasn't she going on and on about some crew agency she was excited about?"

Melody lowers the bong, her nose scrunching up. "Oh yeah." She snaps her fingers. "What was the name?"

"Larry?" the boyfriend tries, scratching his jaw. "*Lair*-y?"

My skin turns cold. I glance at Mrs. Colding—her face has gone pale as bone.

Melody jerks her head. "I think she left the card on the fridge."

I slowly cross to the kitchen. There *is* a business card there. It's pinned to the fridge by a cannabis leaf magnet. Matte cardstock. Expensive-looking. The name of the crew agency on it obscured. I swallow, slowly pull it free so I can read the name . . .

The hairs on my arms stand up. The blood roars in my ears. I look back at Mrs. Colding—she has her hands pressed to the table as if afraid she'll fall. "Let me guess," she says.

"Lair Yachting, Incorporated." Mrs. Colding raises a finely curved eyebrow as she studies the card stamped with RENATA SPROULE, PLACEMENT COORDINATOR. "Do you think . . .?"

I nod. I'm driving us in my rental car through Fort Lauderdale's sun-hazed streets. It's hard to keep the defeat out of my voice. "If she's been missing for a year? Yeah, she's mixed up with their kind." I grit my teeth, my chest rising and falling in sudden, despairing fury that makes me want to pound the steering wheel. Why, Pen? Why yachting? Why Lair Yachting, Inc.? Of all crew agencies in the world . . .

I shake my head, forcing calmness. "I just hope . . ."

Mrs. Colding fixes me with a look. "She's alive. She has to be. And you have a lead now. Lair Yachting should have a record of which boat they placed her on."

I watch her face as she studies the card, so sure of herself. She hasn't changed out of the white button-down and black skirt of a yachtie yet (doing so would, after all, be asking her to give up her identity). Which I'm more than fine with. Because I can never get enough of those legs of hers.

But it's not her legs I'm looking at now. My eyes rest on the fang marks on her neck and I feel a sharp twinge of warning, a tender ache of loss. Because I know what this means for us, now that the Nosferyachtu Club has become involved. And what I have to do.

I take in a deep breath—drawing it out, making the moment last—and smell sandalwood and Asian blossoms.

"Yeah," I say. "I should be able to find her." And I slow to a stop, putting the car in park. "I'll come back for you as soon as I do."

Mrs. Colding blinks at me in confusion, then out the window. Her whole body stiffens when she realizes I've brought her back to Colding Mansion.

"No," she says, her voice dropping. "This doesn't change anything. You're not leaving me here—"

"Oh, but I am." I grip the steering wheel with both hands, as if to keep me to this course. "I won't let you get mixed up in this, too. I won't be responsible for anyone else getting hurt. Least of all you."

A dangerous scowl clouds her face. Then she comports herself, calmly clasping her hands in her lap. I know that look. I know what's coming. I've never wished it on anyone.

She doesn't treat me as an exception whatsoever.

"I'm not your daughter," she intones in a cool, annihilating voice. "And you're not Adrian Voper. You can't fire me. And you sure as hell can't stop me. If you think I'll stay here while you go risk your life to save your daughter alone, then you really don't know me at all, Captain Redfearn."

It's hard not to grin, even in the face of her withering onslaught. It's hard not to be overwhelmed by a sweet swell of gratitude.

But still.

"Look—" I try again.

"Nope." She shakes her head once in a negating swish of her jaw. "If you knew any better, you'd know you can't just waltz into Lair Yachting, Incorporated and expect it to go well. You're a captain in their network—and you're currently persona non grata. Me, on the other hand? A lowly chief stew? A *woman?* They might not recognize me. They might not know me at all. I'm your best bet, Captain Redfearn, whether you like it or not."

Sweet Jesus, she's sexy as hell when she's like this—composed, stubborn, vibrating with fierce loyalty. It's too much. I can't help it.

I lift a hand and tuck one of those flyaway hairs behind her ear.

Everything about her changes. Her breath stills, and a delicate bloom colors her cheeks. But she doesn't look away. She looks, in this moment, almost girlish.

She's the loveliest thing I've ever seen.

"Okay," I say. "But that means we have to put *this*"—I take her hand in mine—"on pause for now." She blushes, looking both flattered and confused, so I go on. "Because if I fall in love with you"—she shivers at the phrase—"I don't know if I can do this. I don't know if I could bear to put you in any danger. If my feelings would be too much of a liability." Her fingers link in mine, feeling as if they've always belonged there, a perfect fit, and our skin sparks at the touch. "We focus on getting my daughter back, and then . . ." I trail off, meeting her eyes. "Deal?"

Her face softens—in hurt, or perhaps disappointment—but she nods her understanding, her mouth easing into a gentle smile. "Deal."

But neither of us moves. We sit there staring into each other's eyes, unable to look away.

FOUR
MRS. COLDING

Captain Redfearn parks the rental car at a discreet distance and we both stare at Lair Yachting, Inc.

I almost couldn't believe the relief I'd felt at leaving Colding Mansion behind, watching it recede in the rearview behind its gate and wall of sickly palm trees. But Lair Yachting has a dark pull all its own. It *lurks*. A squat building of faded stucco and drawn blinds, it looks like something that's wormed its way back into the shadows between the other crew agencies lining Southeast 17th Street—a monstrous malignance hiding in plain sight in the sunny heart of Fort Lauderdale, waiting to bare a sharp grin of cracked plaster ravenous for the flesh of women.

I shiver.

"I don't like this," Captain Redfearn grumbles.

He's been grumpy the whole ride. I can't tell if it's because of what I'm about to do or the decision we've made.

I know which one I hope it is.

I hadn't known how much I'd been looking forward to this until he'd put it on hold. I hadn't known, until that moment, that I'd made my decision. *I was ready.* I was ready to pursue this again, despite all my doubts. Despite the fear in the back of my mind that told me, tauntingly, that it wasn't yet safe to open myself up to that again. Not after Mr. Colding. Not after that.

Nonetheless, I was ready.

And now I'm crushed. He's barely looked at me since we had that conversation, and it sends me into a tumble of doubt. How can he be so detached? Does this not affect him as much as it does me? Is he having second thoughts?

But there's no time for that. I have to concentrate on the matter at hand.

"You ready?" Captain Redfearn asks.

I straighten my spine and nod.

He looks at me, one hand on the wheel, knuckles white and popping with angry veins. His voice is steady with intense focus. "If you think they suspect you? Leave. No hesitation. No second-guessing. Clear?"

I look at him, wanting to put a hand on his knee. Wanting, so badly, to close the distance between us and kiss him. To feel his lips again.

But I hold myself back.

"See you soon," I say and step out of the car before one of us stops me.

A bell tinkles as I open the door to Lair Yachting, Inc.

The skin creeps along my arms. It's dark in here, strikingly so, in contrast to the blazing sun outside. And stale. They need air freshener in here. And a good hoovering. It feels like a mausoleum. The posters on the walls need to be dusted: VISIT ROMANIA! VISIT THE BALTIC RIVIERA! SEE THE CAVES OF SARDINIA!

I shiver. I know the meaning behind those places.

"Can I help you?"

The voice startles me, sending my heart fluttering against my ribs. There's a woman sitting in the dark behind the receptionist's desk, smiling. Her platinum A-line bob gleams like a helmet in the gloom. Her black skirt suit is flawless. She sounds vaguely European, looks vaguely inhuman.

Renata Sproule.

I draw myself up. "Yes." I stride up to the desk. "I'm hiring for a yacht leaving for the Med next week. I was hoping to find a stew in your network. I had a good experience with her on another boat."

"Please, take a seat." Renata Sproule gestures toward a chair, and her nail extensions start clacking on a keyboard. "Name?"

I swallow. Here goes. "Penelope Redfearn."

"Redfearn," the placement coordinator repeats. She glances at me, and my breath stills. There's a mole high on her left cheekbone. It gives her a strangely predatory look.

I smile.

She turns back to her screen. "Our records show she's still employed on a boat."

A brief feeling of relief unfurls inside me. "How disappointing." I brush a piece of lint off my skirt, my voice carefully neutral. "And what boat was that?"

She blinks at me.

I shrug. "Maybe I can persuade them to give her up."

Farther back in the gloom of the crew agency, there's a click—a door opening.

My pulse knocks in my ears. I look up to see two shapes emerging from the shadows. One is dark-skinned, muscular and wears a white polo with the gold epaulettes of a captain, the other a brushed wool suit, his skin very pale against the navy fabric. It seems to float through that dimness with the ghostly luminescence of a moon.

The two men are walking down the hall to the waiting room. Toward me.

"We're glad to have you aboard," the pale-faced man says in a cool, cultured voice, stopping to shake the yachtie's hand. There's a white glint of sharpness to his smile. "The Commodore wants the *Lair*'s captain tracked down as soon as possible."

My stomach bottoms out. A high-pitched whine fills my ears.

They're talking about Captain Redfearn.

The doorbell tinkles, and as he turns away the pale-faced man glances at me and pauses. I quickly avert my gaze. It's hard to breathe. My heart feels like it wants to beat out of my chest. Has he recognized me?

Then . . .

"I'll be in back, Miss Sproule," the man says after a moment, striding back into the shadows. "Let me know when it's sundown."

"Of course, sir," Renata Sproule replies in a clipped, professional voice. She does not turn her head when she says it. She's watching me, stiff and faced away in my seat. Her eyes narrow. "Do I know you?"

A light sweat is on my skin now. It's very cold. It's also very hard to concentrate with the fear drumming away inside me. I force myself to look at her. "I don't think so, no."

Her stare continues, and I wonder what will happen if she calls for that creature in the back office. I wonder if I'll be able to get to her before she does. Get out the door before—

"Well," Renata Sproule says with a smirk, taking in my face, the shape of my eyes. "It's hard to tell you people apart, isn't it?" And she turns back to her screen.

Dull shock lodges in my gut. It's only my years of training that keeps my jaw from dropping. *That little . . .*

More keys tap, more nails clack. Renata Sproule lifts her nose and announces, without looking at me, "The boat is called the *Thing*."

When I leave Lair Yachting, Inc., there's no sign of that other captain. The only captain to be seen is Redfearn, standing anxiously by the gleaming rental car. Relief floods through me, leaving me weak. I all but run across the street to him.

"Jesus, I was getting worried," he says.

"*You* were worried?" I return, stopping myself from touching him. "That other captain who came out? He was hired to hunt you down. The Commodore wants to punish everyone connected to Adrian."

This doesn't seem to throw him at all. "We can deal with that," he assures me. He dips his head to catch my gaze. "Did you . . .?"

I nod, once, then again and again, unable to stop myself from smiling. I simply can't when he's like this; he's like a little boy. He lets out a gush of laughter, overjoyed, brimming over with happiness, and grabs my face in his big hands. "You beautiful thing," he says and plants a kiss full on my lips.

It takes him a moment to realize what he's done. His whole body stiffens. When he pulls back, we both stare. His eyes have flown wide, glassy with astonishment. I can feel his breath on my face, see every fleck of color in his gray eyes. My heart is beating faster than it did back in Lair Yachting, Inc. And I think, *Please don't stop.*

He carefully lets my face go and takes a step back, harrumphing deep in his throat.

My body feels that retreat like a physical loss. I flutter my gaze away, filled with a strange mixture of hope and humiliation as he palms his neck and looks at his deck shoes. A strange and bittersweet celebration.

So it's not just me, then.

"Well," he gruffs. "Did you—did you get the name of the captain? Of Penelope's boat?"

I nod, my lips still tingling. It's hard to use them, to think of using them for anything else than for what just happened. "Seamus Murdoch."

He jerks at me. "Seamus?"

I blink. "You know him?"

He looks past me at the ominous front of Lair Yachting, slow with thought. "Yeah," he says. "Yeah, I do."

FIVE

CAPTAIN REDFEARN

Officially, it's Waxy O'Connor's Irish Pub, but all the yachties call it Waxy's.

It's also a favorite haunt of the yacht captains.

I sit in my cracked-leather booth and listen to all the South African yachties and expat rugby fans go crazy over the match on the TV. It's a rowdy night, and the dark-wood bar is packed. I can hardly hear myself think. I glance at Mrs. Colding perched on a stool at the bar, looking cool and put-together and stunningly out of place amongst the raucous sports fans. We'd agreed I should meet my old chum alone, and that she should come but keep her distance. If I'm really persona non grata, then we don't want to risk her getting spotted with me. No point in needlessly endangering her.

She's not particularly overjoyed at the choice of venue, though. She leans away, nose wrinkled, as the rugby fan beside her explodes, screaming invectives at the TV. She catches my eye, brow lifted, and I grin before my ears turn red and I rub my forehead, pervaded by a squirming embarrassment and regret. What was I doing? Why did I kiss her? Did I scare her off after I told her we'd wait?

Damn, it's almost enough to make me drink the whiskey in front of me.

I haven't had a drink in years. Not since I began working for Adrian. Not since I ended my international bar crawl over losing Penelope. This one's for Seamus.

But it attracts my attention the more I look at it. It sits in front of me like a smooth, golden brown gulp of temptation. The sight of it makes my mouth go dry, my palms sweat.

I'm thinking of what it would feel like to have that familiar, exquisite burn going down my throat when Seamus Murdoch sidles out of the crowd.

Something in me goes cold. He used to be the spitting image of an Irish sea captain—stout and ruddy-cheeked, with a mane of curly red hair. Now? He's gone sallow, gaunt as a ghoul with a day's growth of stubble, and his fiery hair is limp and thinning, its luster gone. He looks like a bundle of sticks inside his white captain's polo; I hardly recognize him. And I know him as few souls can know one another. I've known him since I entered the yachting industry as a wary twenty-six-year-old fresh out of the Navy. We ended up in the same crew house and became inseparable, two unruly lads fleeing the shadows of their fathers. We made a pact together. We'd get hired on the same boat and log our sea hours, work our way up to captain, achieve our dream of one day running our own boats. We thought we'd make our fortunes, become the men we always wanted to be—the men our fathers never were. Little did we know that's exactly what our fathers thought they were doing, too.

"Christ, Seamus," I say as he slips into the booth opposite me. "What happened to you?"

He doesn't seem to hear me. He keeps twitching about, glancing over his shoulder as if afraid he's been followed. Then he notices the whiskey I'm pushing toward him and promptly knocks it back, wipes his mouth and signals for another. He won't quite look at me. "Jaysis, it's quare crowded in here, innit?" he says in his thick Irish brogue. He's rocking back and forth, his hands clasped on the table, bopping up and down.

"Seamus," I say.

"Haven't seen you in donkey's years," he says to himself, a little too loud, still not looking at me. "Gettin' your call . . . it put the heart crossway in me, it did. S'like ya knew or somethin'." On the TV, a team scores and the rugby fans explode into cheers. Seamus jumps, looking as if he's about to hyperventilate.

I reach out and put my hand on his. "Seamus," I say, grounding him. "What's going on?"

When he finally looks at me, tears fill his eyes. "I didn't know," he blubbers. "I swear on me mum's grave I didn't know . . ."

A chill works its way down to the base of my spine. I glance at Mrs. Colding, who's watching us with a worried pinch between her brows. "Know what?"

Seamus taps his fingertips on the table, lowers his voice and leans in. "When she came to me, she made me promise not to tell ya. She just wanted to be a stewardess. Try to prove somethin' to ya. And back then I didn't know what I was gettin' into . . ."

An old, dark anger coils in my gut. "Just spit it out, Seamus."

The Irish captain waits for his whiskey, drains it in one go and sighs, a fortifying, teeth-together sound, and runs a hand through his lank red hair. "The boat I skipper—"

"The *Thing*."

He nods. "She does milk runs to a place that ain't on no map. Some hidden location in the arse end of the South China Sea. It's where Penelope—" His eyes tear up again.

My hand closes into a fist on the table. "What happened?"

"You'll never get her back," he whispers.

The anger hums all along beneath my skin now. I have to keep my voice from rising. "What is this place? What *happened*, goddamn it?"

He looks up at me. "It's his base."

My hide prickles. "His *what?* Whose?"

"The Commodore's. It's Volok's base."

For a moment, I don't think I've heard right. "The Commodore—these fucks have *boats*, not fucking—"

"I had no choice," Seamus goes on. "You understand?" His eyes beseech me. "There's someone there who acts as caretaker while Volok's gone. They call him 'the Steward.'"

My blood runs cold.

"He . . . *claimed* her." Seamus' face screws up as the tears begin to leak out of his eyes. "I'd no choice, Arnold," he says again. "You have to believe me. You any idea what they'd do to me if I said anythin'?" His shoulders begin to rise and fall as the panic twists at him. "I didn't know what to do, didn't know how to tell you . . ." He covers his face with his hands.

I lean back against the booth, feeling as if my insides have been scraped out. Mrs. Colding knows something is wrong. I can feel her watching me, anxious, half off her stool, debating to break cover and cross the room to me. But I hold out a hand under the table, a warning: *No.* The queasy feeling of betrayal is sinking in now. Seamus had always been a bit squirrely, at times hard to depend on, but *this* . . . Volok's base. The Steward. My daughter. *Penelope*. It doesn't make any sense. It can't make sense. This can't have happened. I can't have caused this.

But I have.

I lean forward, that old anger muscling its way up from the darkness, wanting an outlet. I keep my voice steady. "Take me with you."

But Seamus goes ashen-faced with horror. "No," he breathes, shaking his head. "I cain't. I—I resigned—"

Condiments and glasses go flying as I lunge across the table and grab him by the shirt, haul him halfway out of his seat so we're face to face. "Then you'll make it up to me," I grit through clenched teeth, "and put me up for the new captaincy."

Out of the corner of my eye, Mrs. Colding jolts to her feet, face white with fear.

Seamus sags in my hands, oozing guilt. "Cain't," he whispers.

"Why not?" I growl.

"Because another captain's already replaced me."

All that anger in me drains away. I release him and slump back into my seat, a tight numbness in my chest.

"I couldn't do it no more," Seamus explains and holds up his hands—they're quivering. "I got the shakes. I cain't sleep. Every night I see—I see—"

I don't hear him anymore. A great hopelessness descends on me, sapping me of all will, leaving me in a state of dumb shock. This is followed by an angry cinder of defiance: No. This can't be it. There has to be a way. As a superyacht captain, this is what you're paid for—to provide the impossible.

Then it comes to me.

"Has the Steward seen the face of this new captain?" I blurt.

Seamus blinks at me. "What?"

"Would he recognize him?"

Seamus' brows draw together. "No, but—"

I can't help it: I grin a wolfish grin, dangerous, triumphant and without humor. "Then you'll tell me where the boat is docked," I growl, meeting his eyes, "and I'll find a way to replace this new captain."

SIX

MRS. COLDING

"I'm so sorry," I whisper as the elevator takes us up.

Captain Redfearn nods and shrugs the strap of his duffel bag higher up on his shoulder. "I know."

I feel as if there's a great emptiness in my stomach. I don't feel anything. All the words following the phrase "She's been taken" have blurred into a great roar of noise. I feel sick. Lightheaded. Only the mention of China gets through.

China. I'm going back to China.

I'm going home.

The elevator doors ding open and Captain Redfearn strides out into the dim motel hallway. I trail behind him, mustering words. "So how do you plan on replacing this captain?"

"No idea," he grunts. He glances at his room key, at the numbers on the doors lining the hall.

I'm almost afraid to ask it. "Have you thought about what you might have to resort to?"

The muscles in Redfearn's shoulders tighten. "Yeah," he gruffs. "I have." He stabs his key into a door and unlocks it, pushes inside and stops. "Shit."

It's a typical Fort Lauderdale hotel room. Long, airy, with a private balcony overlooking the bay. The first thing I check for is how clean it is. But I know what's caught Captain Redfearn's attention.

It's the bed. The queen-sized bed. The *only* bed in the room.

I feel my chest flush hot as Captain Redfearn drops his bag and strides to the phone on the nightstand, dials for service. "Hello?" he says. "This is room three eleven. I asked for two beds." He stands there a moment as I wring my hands, feeling that heat spread into my cheeks, my ears, turning everything pink. He places a hand on his hip. "Uh-huh. No other rooms available, then." He glances at me, his stubbled jaw clenching, and turns away. "Fine. No. No, thank you." He clicks the phone back down, a little too sharply, and I think how I've never seen this kind of anger in him before. I'd half-expected him to strangle that shifty Irishman back in the bar, and it would've been startling though understandable. This anger at our predicament is different, though—I can't help but feel a warm glow at what it means. I feel almost dizzy.

"We could go somewhere else—" I offer.

But he sighs and runs a hand down his face. "It's late. I'll sleep on the floor." He glances at my bag, at the bathroom, and his throat dips in a swallow as he gestures. "I'll let you—"

That heat again. I must be turning a furious red by now. I nod and sweep into the bathroom before he can see it, shut the door behind me and lean against it. My heart is jumping in my chest. What is wrong with me? He's turned me into a blushing teenager. I shake my head and change out of my yachtie shirt and skirt, slip into my set of silver silk pajamas. Then I brush my teeth, splash water on my face.

Only one thing left. There's no getting around it.

I pull out the pins in my immaculate bun, gather up my silky black hair and secure it into a topknot with a tie. I consider myself in the mirror for a long moment. It's unbearably messy. Nothing like my flawless do during the day. I feel naked.

God, he's going to laugh.

I hesitate a long moment with my hand on the knob of the bathroom door, a shiver passing through me. This is ridiculous. I'm being a fool.

I turn the knob and step out.

He's standing before the open sliding glass door leading out onto the balcony, staring out at the rippling black of the sea. I square my shoulders.

"You're not allowed to poke fun," I warn him. "My hair gets damaged if I don't—"

But when he turns around, the change in his face halts all words in my throat. His eyes go wide. They travel down every inch of me, soaking me in as if I were wearing lingerie instead of a full-length set of pajamas, then up to my crazy nest of hair, and a gentle smile curls his lips. It's not a mocking smile. It's something altogether different.

I find my breathing has become erratic.

"I know better than to ever poke fun at you, Mrs. Colding," he says in a solemn tone.

It's very hard to fight back a smile as I turn away. "Good," I admonish, feeling my cheeks go red again. I go to the bed, feeling his eyes on me, and I'm suddenly very aware of how tight these pajama bottoms are—and what they're showcasing. I'm not as young as I once was. Is the light in here forgiving? Will he think my buttocks droop more than a younger woman's? Can he see the outline of my lacy black panties under the silk . . . and do I want him to?

The air is filling up with possibilities. We're in a hotel room. Alone. And there's only one bed. How am I to sleep tonight? How will either of us sleep tonight?

I don't know what to do with all this nervous energy. Before I know it, I'm tugging at the sheets of the bed. "Look at this," I mutter, tucking them back in yachtie-style. "No standards. No standards at all."

I feel the solid weight of a body behind me. It's Captain Redfearn, and his mouth is crooked in a white smile that's telling me a hundred things. The warmth radiates off him like a stove. He seems to be everywhere.

He touches my arm. "It's okay," his voice rumbles behind me. "We're not on a boat."

I still all over. My breath has caught in my throat. I'm shuddering, my skin going tingly with goose bumps. I can feel his body almost touching mine. I feel as if I am on a precipice, caught between two warring impulses.

I tug at the sheet. "Someone has to uphold standards."

He smirks, grabs one of the pillows and lies down on the floor, punches the pillow under his head. "You always clean when you're nervous?"

"Hush," I say and he chuckles as I lift up the duvet and dive inside the cool clean sheets, shivering at the feeling. Then I turn over in bed to stare down at him, one hand propped against my cheek. I feel almost drunk, ready to reveal another version of myself. I feel as if anything can now be possible. This is what he's done to me.

Then he says something that makes my scalp constrict. "Did it start with Mr. Colding?"

I blink at him, all breath stopped in my lungs.

He watches me with solemn eyes. "Did he make you feel like you had to be perfect at everything?"

I have a sudden desire to bolt, to shrink away from the sudden sensation of having my deepest self exposed. I settle for hedging. "Maybe," I say. "Maybe it's the only way I feel I have control over my life."

He seems to consider this, his eyes searching my face. I feel caught between wanting to hide and to reach out and feel his stubble under my hand. It's utterly terrifying.

"And how do you feel," he says, "going back to your home country?"

A strange ache twists my stomach. "I don't know," I reply in all honesty. Then, impish, "But that's none of your business, Captain Redfearn."

He smirks. "When are we going to call each other by our first names?"

I contemplate that one. "I don't know," I say. "I don't know how I'd think of myself if I wasn't a yachtie."

He nods, having expected that. The fact that he had already known the answer before he asked makes my heart ache now. When I speak, my whisper is almost a plea. "You sure you're comfy down there?"

Our eyes lock, and the invitation in that question hovers in the air between us. Then his gray eyes grow sad, kind. "I'm all right," he says.

The hurt is like the breathtaking slide of a knife blade between my ribs—but expected. I nod, roll onto my back and we both stare up at the ceiling, listening to the hissing crawl of the sea on the beach below.

I understand. I do. He's going through so much, after all.

"How are you doing with all this?" I say to the ceiling.

He's silent on the floor for a long moment. "I'm okay," he replies at last, the words thick in his throat.

I lie there, my heart beating very fast in my chest. Slowly, very slowly, I let my arm slide off the edge of the bed, my hand dangle down.

After a moment, he takes it.

"She'll be okay," I say, squeezing hard. "We'll find her. I promise."

His answering squeeze is full of desperate strength. "Thank you, Mrs. Colding."

"You're welcome, Captain Redfearn."

We lie there for a long while holding each other's hand as the waves sigh up onto the shore, counting down the moments until we find Penelope Redfearn.

CAPTAIN'S LOG

Lantau to Hibernacula, December 7th.
Ship: *Golden Sun.*
Speed: 30 knots.
Distance: 18 mi.
Weather: Clear, calm night.
Notes: Flight takes a day to Hong Kong. Then the afternoon to hire a boat on Lantau. I inspect the fuel level, hull, propeller, navigation lights, anchors, fenders, fittings while Mrs. Colding finishes paperwork. Then I write this log entry. Gives me time to think. Seamus gave me coordinates to the *Thing*'s location. Only heard rumors of the place. Know it's owned by Nosferyachtu Club and little else.

They call it Hibernacula.

I won't think of what may be required soon. Can't do that yet. And I don't want to picture it. What that Steward may be doing to you. What may have drove you to this. Makes my stomach heave.

All this has been making me think of you more. Things I haven't thought of in years, bubbling up from the past. I'm thinking of when you were six years old. You had the whooping cough and I was staying up all night with you. Making sure you were sitting upright in bed so you wouldn't drown in your own vomit. I'd never been so scared in my life. You must have known, because you looked at me and said, I won't die daddy. And I said, I know. And you said, Will you die someday? And I said, Yes. And you said, Where will you go? And I said, I don't know. And you said, Will you find your way back to me? And I said, Yes. And you said, How? And I said, Because you're my little sun. You can always find your way back to the sun. And you put your hand in my hand and said, Yes, as if it had been decided.

I had to ask your mother to watch you so you wouldn't see me cry.

I'm so sorry. Sorry I let myself lose you. Sorry I put your mother through this. She doesn't deserve it. This is on me.

Maybe she'll see you again. Maybe I can bring you back to her, even if you don't want to see me. It's the least I can do for what I did to our marriage. To her.

Yes. I can do that. And maybe—maybe—I'll feel your hand in mine again.

I'm coming, Pen. I'm on the trail now. I will find you. I will save you from this Steward.

You're my little sun.

SEVEN
MRS. COLDING

As the rigid inflatable boat chugs across the glittering waters of Victoria Harbour, I blink away the spray beading my lashes and gaze up in disbelief.

I'd almost forgotten how beautiful it is: Hong Kong is an enchantment of light.

It's a nightscape of fiery neon and towers clad in reflective glass. Advertisements scroll across soaring skyscrapers: glowering Chinese calligraphy, blooming flowers, smiling women. It all rises against the night like a giant dream of seduction.

Home.

It all rushes back to me. The evenings spent sneaking out to the night markets in Kowloon, wiping the grease from shish kabobs on my traditional qipao while I strolled past the shop windows full of Western clothing I thought I'd never wear, women I thought I'd never be. Going fishing with my father in his old trawler among the verdant outlying islands, learning how to tie a knot while my blood sang in response to his ancient folk songs. The day everything changed when my father introduced me

to a strange American who'd paid for a tour on the water
. . .

"You okay?"

The low voice startles me, and I turn to look at Captain Redfearn at the helm. "Yes," I say, and give him a wan smile. "It's . . . I never thought I'd come back here."

He nods, gray eyes crinkled as he studies me. "This is where you met Mr. Colding, isn't it?"

I can still see my father's face as he leaned down to kiss my brow in goodbye. *Never forget who you are.*

"No," I say, looking down at my Western clothes, my yachtie shirt and skirt, then back up at the pulsing lights of Hong Kong. "It's where I left behind who I used to be."

I can feel Captain Redfearn's eyes on my back, but he doesn't pursue this remark. He's turning the wheel hand over hand, swinging us away from the dazzling waterfront of Hong Kong. He compares the string of coordinates he wrote on his wrist to his chart plotter, threads us through the crush of boats choking the harbor: ferries with their running lights, Chinese junks with their red beams and sails. Soon, we're leaving the neon-bathed glow of Hong Kong behind, heading out to darker waters. It's quieter out here. More mysterious. A place of mists and shadows. Out on the horizon, I see a black hump getting closer. It's what we're heading toward.

It's an island.

It's darker than the other outlying islands in the bay. Only a smattering of lights out there. As we near, I understand why. The only landmark on that island is a single, dilapidated warehouse of breathtaking scale, a lurid splash of neon calligraphy across its hangar doors with a translation in English beneath: HIBERNACULA MARINE STORAGE. All about it crowds the dark immensity of a forest, its tropical lushness all but exuding a green mist that seems about to engulf the building.

For a moment, my father is beside me again, pouring warnings into my twelve-year-old ear: *Stay away from that island*.

I shiver.

I'd forgotten the dark lore surrounding that place. The whispers of both children and old fishermen. They'd said it was cursed.

But then, I've always been drawn toward what's ruined me.

There's a row of boat slips before the warehouse, a marina alive with the dark shapes of cranes and boat hoists. But Captain Redfearn doesn't go for that. He kills the RIB's lights, noses us into a shallow cove hidden from the marina behind a clump of boulders. After we secure the boat, we creep through the dense undergrowth until we have a view of the warehouse again.

It's even bigger up close. It looks like it could house a battleship. Its black paint is flecked and peeling, its signage ten feet tall. A red neon "R" flickers and blinks on and off in a lonely buzz of voltage.

In that flickering light, two bulky, black-suited men can be seen standing before the doors of the warehouse, hands clasped before them.

Security guards.

"Shit," Captain Redfearn breathes.

There's the hum of an engine, and we both turn. A lean, Italian-looking man in a slick cream suit is hopping out of a powerboat in one of the boat slips. He strides across the concrete marina with an air of utter boredom, dips a hand into his breast pocket and removes a passport. One of the security guards checks it, hands it back. "Enjoy your sleep, Mr. Polidori."

One of the hangar doors rolls back a few feet, exposing a strip of darkness three stories tall, and the man in the cream suit disappears inside.

My skin has gone cold. *Enjoy your sleep?*

Captain Redfearn, similarly, is less than excited. "So I just need the passport of a man I don't even know how to find?" he grunts, and runs a hand down his face. "Perfect."

But something's caught my attention: the pilot who'd delivered the man in the cream suit. He's ashore now, too. He's dressed in khaki shorts and a white polo with four gold stripes on the shoulders: a yachtie captain. And he's rounding the warehouse.

Before I know what I'm doing, I've left our hiding spot to get a better view.

Captain Redfearn's fingers swipe after me. "Hey!" He joins me behind a parked forklift, just as I see the captain enter—

"What the hell?" Redfearn hisses. "What are you—"

And I turn his head with both hands so he can see: a small jet-black building hunched in the shadow of the warehouse, its garish neon sign above the door in both Chinese and English lettering: *Captain's Club*.

It's hard not to smirk. "I think I know where we'll find our captain."

If I'd been expecting Captain Redfearn to be happy about this, I was wrong. All color goes from his face. He stares at the bar as if at a ghost from the past, and I remember: *Ah*.

Redfearn swallows hard. "Stay by the boat," he says without looking at me. "I'll be back soon."

I bristle. "Why—" I begin, and then my blood chills as I stare at *Captain's Club* buzzing in the night. "Oh. I see. No girls allowed."

Almost angrily, he nods.

I feel my cheeks flushing, an inexplicable embarrassment flooding me. I force it down and blurt, "Won't they recognize you?"

He shakes his head. "Adrian was a lone wolf. I haven't rubbed elbows with many of the Nosferyachtu Club captains." He shrugs. "I'll just have to hope none of them know what I look like."

He settles his shoulders, preparing himself—he's about to go. I touch his arm. "You going to be all right in there?" I hesitate. "Alone?"

At this, he tears his eyes from the bar as if coming back from a faraway place. Then he winces a smile. It's terrible.

"What's your plan?" I say, trying to get something—anything—out of him.

But he only touches the backs of his fingers to my cheek. "I'll see you soon," he promises, the gentleness in his tone squeezing my throat shut. Then he's striding across the marina floor toward the *Captain's Club* of Hibernacula, leaving me waiting in the shadows with dull dread filling my veins like lead.

EIGHT

CAPTAIN REDFEARN

When I step inside the *Captain's Club*, all the old memories gust into me like a wind.

Returning to Waxy's hadn't brought them on. Perhaps it had been too clean, too nice, too connected to good times. But this—this is a dive bar. This is like all the other dives I'd haunted around the world, back when I'd been trying my damnedest to drink myself to death. This is the kind of place where I'd felt I belonged—where the worthless came to rot. There's the same stickiness of spilled beer on the floor. The same dim lighting, courtesy here of ornate paper lanterns, the better to hide your shame. There's also the same obligatory kitsch, given the unique flavor here of Far East pirate den, with a touch of the eerie from the faded painting above the bar depicting coffins being loaded onto Chinese junks against a burning sky. There's even the drunk puking in the corner, and I think of all the nights when I'd gone too far, when my crewmates had given up trying to drag me back to the boat and left me to stew in my swill of self-hatred, cursing and crying . . .

Welcome back, Arnold.

I realize I'm gathering attention and approach the long wrap-around bar, lean my elbows on the dark red wood and wait for the bartender as I covertly scan the clientele. Polo-wearing figures fill the place, hunched on barstools or tucked into bloodred leather booths. The details, at first, are in keeping with the sailors I've been around all my life. Hair cropped short. Tans that evoke weathered leather. Faint white traceries of scars.

But then I notice other things.

The brute next to me, for example, has long red scratches on his forearms and face, and a chill coils around the base of my spine. Claw marks. Those are claw marks. Those are from the fingernails of women.

The conversations around me begin to filter into my ears.

"Told me to drop anchor in Karpathos, leave him ashore with the women . . ."

"Could hear the screams all night . . ."

"You wouldn't believe the blood . . ."

"Asked me to hold her down . . ."

"Said, Did I want to join in?"

My heart, I find, is pounding in my chest. I hadn't known how lucky I'd had it with Adrian. These guys make my pals at Waxy's seem quaint.

These are the rotten ones.

"You want drink?"

I startle and look up. The bartender, a Chinese man of indeterminate age in a white suit and black bowtie, eyes me expectantly.

I swallow hard, taking in the rows of bottles on the backbar. My old friends. There's the familiar black label of Jack Daniels, my closest confidante, my dark lover. Her pull is almost gravitational, promising oblivion. *You can stop here*, her amber body whispers. *This is where you belong. Would Penelope want you back, anyway?*

I squeeze my eyes shut before I can't, take a deep breath.

"Just—do you know Captain Malter, by chance?"

The bartender blinks at this, as if disappointed. Then turns and points.

There's a line of men snaking out the restroom. The last of them is about my age and has my silver hair, the kind of frat bro beefiness and good looks that often turns to fat. Even if he weren't a bit unsteady, I'd still know him to be a heavy drinker. It's the eyes. They're hot and bloodshot. I once had those eyes.

He's the subject of conversation amongst the captains.

"You're shitting me," one of them says as I approach. "The Steward? The *Steward* hired you?"

Malter lifts his hands in a smug articulation of *What can I say?*

"And what the fuck makes you qualified? Everyone here has worked boats that size."

"He knows how to keep his mouth shut, for one," another captain drawls.

"And not everyone has Malter's taste in things," yet another says under his breath.

Malter, in reply, smooches a juicy kiss at him.

"Still," the smartass captain says, louder now, coming to his point. "Ain't exactly jealous. We all know how long the Steward's captains last . . ."

And that's my cue.

"I'll take the gig off your hands," I announce, planting myself behind Captain Malter.

The men in line glance at me, including Malter. A brow lifts with enough attitude to be sentient.

I shrug. "I wouldn't mind proving myself to the Commodore."

Malter gives me a once-over. His lips are too soft, too pink. They make me think of a petulant child. "You know what the Steward would do to me if I backed out now?" he huffs. "You think he's ever gonna stop hunting that Irish shit-weasel who walked out on him?"

That fear coils around my spine again.

I fumble for a reply, for one last way to convince this douche. This can't be it. There has to be a way to get through to him, to not resort to—

But there isn't.

Malter cranes his head at the line, does that little side-to-side shuffle that tells you he can't wait much longer, and it comes to me.

"Better take it outside before you piss yourself," I grunt, jutting my chin at Captain Malter's shorts. He squints a hard look at me, and I shrug a shoulder, gesture. "No line out there."

He glances at the line, settles for a sneer. "Yeah, fuck this," he mutters and brushes past me for the door, leaving me standing there watching after him—filled with resignation and foreboding.

I step outside into the red wash of the *Captain's Club*'s neon sign and scan the night. I can see the shaggy heads of palm trees against the stars, a vast wall of darkness. Something rumbles by, beeping, and I turn to see a forklift, a powerboat poised on its long, spear-like forks, impossibly huge. Then it's rumbled past me into the shadows beyond the glow of the warehouse lights. If I squint, I can glimpse a presence in those shadows, tall metallic shapes, rigid and ordered: racks. Rows of powerboats stacked four tall on open racks of high-quality structural steel. Hundreds of them. A whole graveyard of them. A boatel. As I watch, the forklift lifts its forks and deposits its load into a high berth.

Captain Malter stands down one of those dark aisles, his back faintly red from the neon lights, letting out a steaming arc of piss with a sigh.

I swallow and follow him into the dark.

It's very still, this night. Very quiet. I case the marina to make sure—not a soul about. No one to witness what's about to happen. Especially Mrs. Colding.

As I go, I stoop down to pick up a stray concrete brick used to prop up smaller boats. It feels heavy and functional in my hand.

I am very close now. I stop two paces behind him. He hasn't heard me.

I tell myself this is what's required. That this has to happen.

This is how I get my Penelope.

A flash of light catches my attention, and I jolt my gaze over Malter's shoulder. There's a figure standing in the shadows there. My muscles lock. My skin breaks out in goosepimples. I can't be seeing what I am seeing, but I am. A goggled face, a sleek black wetsuit and tactical rifle held across the chest. The panes of the diving goggles flash at me, and I don't need to see the eyes behind them to know that they're my own.

The old me nods, giving permission: You can be that again.

Again. They come back to me now: the kills. Sneaking through the surf of foreign shores, rising dripping out of jungle rivers like a green-painted nightmare. My bullets taking soldiers in the throat, my knife planted in skulls, my bicep choking off windpipes, that old dark rage in me focused to a metallic purpose . . .

This is what you have to be again to get her back.

My breathing has gotten slow and heavy. My teeth clench. My eyes and nostrils burn, everything inside me in revolt.

Captain Malter sways and grunts, the patter of piss trailing away to a trickle. Not much time.

My trembling hand lifts the brick—

And Malter lifts his phone, the glow of its screen startling in the dark, and opens up his camera roll.

They're photos of a woman's face. A young woman's face.

The brick freezes in the air.

No. He has a daughter. A family. Guilt rips through me, violent as a knife wound. I can't do this. I can't be that again.

The Navy SEAL apparition watches as I lower the brick.

No.

And I stiffen as Captain Malter continues to scroll.

The photos change. More photos of a young woman. Of young *women*. They wear stewardess outfits, look at the camera with coy smiles, mouths open in laughter. Soon the clothes come off, the women crawl onto beds. Then the blood comes. Blood splattered all over the women and sheets in shocking gouts of red. The women screaming, becoming still, eyes dull and staring. Other shapes now, hunched over them. Feeding.

Not his daughter. Not his daughter.

I can hear Malter's breathing now. It's gotten deeper, irregular. The hand not holding the phone is working back and forth in quick succession, accompanied by a fapping sound.

Good God. This is his kink. *He's getting off on this*. This is why he does the job.

Everything I see turns red.

And Captain Malter glances over his shoulder and sees me holding the brick.

"The *fuck?*" he says, his expression slackening in anger and stupid disbelief, and my response is pure instinct—I swing the brick in a brutal haymaker and smash it across his skull.

The blow staggers him to one knee, his phone shattering on the concrete in a crisp spiderwebbing of glass. I gape. He feels the wound with a trembling hand, the blood matting the hair there, spurting in a thin arc from the scalp. "Mother*fucker!*" he says, dragging his voice out of him in a beastly snarl. "The *fuck* you do to me?"

I look about in a panic. The marina looks deserted. But wait—the door to the *Captain's Club* is opening and I hear voices, someone is coming out—

Malter pushes himself up onto both feet again, blood dripping in braiding rivulets down his face now, turning it into a deranged mask. "You," he says, reaching into his pocket.

"Please," I whisper, lifting a conciliatory hand. "Just—just please be quiet—"

The voices grow louder. Closer. They're going to hear.

There's the flash of something sharp in Malter's hand and everything inside me goes cold and clinical and I think, *This is what you have to be.*

And then—

"Malter! The fuck are you?"

Malter and I lock eyes.

He opens his mouth to shout, but I don't give him time—I hurl the brick full force into his face.

It drops him like a stone. I hear the sickening crunch of cartilage, the wet buckling of bone, but I don't take any chances. In a moment I'm on him, rolling onto my back with my arm around his neck, my bicep hooked under his chin and squeezing his windpipe, Malter flopping on top of me like a fish.

"The *fuck*, Malter?" My blood freezes over as footsteps stop dangerously close. A voice calls out into the dark aisle. "You pass out in there again?"

I squeeze harder against Malter's windpipe, cutting off all sound, and school my voice into something appropriately douchey. "Just gimme a goddamn minute!" I manage between pants, twisting away from Malter's hands clawing at my face. "Fucking pissed myself!"

Silence. I hold my breath, arms locked, listening, praying they can't hear Malter's deck shoes kicking at the concrete—

And there's a scornful snort as the footsteps fade away. "Fucking Malter."

I wait until Malter's weak struggles have stilled before I let out an explosive, gasping breath of relief and revulsion, push the body off me and scrabble away from it. Sweat has broken out all over my body. I feel lightheaded, sick to my stomach. Yes. I'm going to be sick.

The hot surge in my throat brings me to all fours and I spew vomit everywhere. I close my eyes and wait for the nausea to pass, trembling and feverish. I hold a hand to my eyes. I breathe.

When I look up, there's no frogman standing like a rubber-clad specter in the shadows. I'm alone.

Operation successful.

I sit down hard on my ass, hands braced on the concrete on either side of me, and try to take stock. I did it. I did what I swore I'd never do again. I know that if I'm not careful, the guilt—the wrenching shock of what I've done—will overwhelm me. I can't afford that right now. Now for what is far harder than the act itself: the doing away of what has happened. I need to shove this memory far down into a dark corner of my mind, compartmentalize it, keep it forever from myself and Mrs. Colding. I don't know if that can be done, if I am still capable of such a feat, if I ever fully was. All I know is, I have to think about next steps. The body. I have to get rid of the body. The cold, unavoidable fact of this brings me to my feet. First, I go through the clothes, then grab the body's arms and pull. Christ, I'd forgotten how heavy a dead body is. There's no way I can get him to the water. That's at least a hundred yards off.

I cast about for a solution. There's a powerboat resting on chocks not ten feet from me. That'll work.

I haul Malter to it, get his upper body flopped over the side, tip him in. A spare tarp from a nearby pontoon does the job of covering the body.

Then I find a forklift.

Someone has the left the keys in the ignition. The driving is the easy part. It takes a moment to get the right levers working so I can manipulate the forks, scoop

Malter's powerboat-as-coffin off its chocks. Then more rumbling as I bear it away down an aisle of racked boats, looking for a high berth.

There's one at the end. Perfect.

I scrape the boat up a bit getting it in, but that's all right. Hopefully, by the time they find the body—that is, by the time the birds get at it, or the smell becomes too rank—I'll have already found Penelope.

All that's left now is to drag my hands down my face, erase every trace of what I have done.

Mrs. Colding is waiting in the shadows where I left her. She straightens when she sees me striding into the wash of light from the warehouse, her voice a gush of relief. "Captain Redfearn?"

"No," I reply, and hold up the license I got off the body. "It's Captain Malter now."

NINE

MRS. COLDING

"Well?" I ask, a deep unease twisting my gut as we approach the warehouse. "How did it go?"

Captain Redfearn takes a moment, his eyes not quite meeting mine. A band of muscle in his temple pulses. "I . . . *persuaded* him."

My pace falters, my skin going cold as I glance back into the shadows of the boat racks.

No. Don't think about that. Not yet.

A buzzing grows—that flickering neon letter above us. The guards are ahead. Very pale, eyes hidden behind black shades, hair shaved close to the sides of their heads to reveal colorful tattoos, a swirling parade of mythical creatures—Triad members, by the looks of them.

Captain Redfearn stops before them.

After a moment, a hand is held out, inked to look as taloned as its employers.

Redfearn places Malter's 100 Ton Master Captain's License into it.

Sweat slicks my palms as the security guard flips through the little leather book embossed in gold foil, black-inked fingers thumbing through the stiff paper. He stops on Malter's photo and glances up at Redfearn.

Redfearn swallows, shrugs. "I've lost weight."

My mouth has gone dry. The black shades turn to me.

"My chief stew," Redfearn croaks helpfully.

The two security guards glance at each other. No word spoken. Then the one with the license jerks his head and his fellow walks off toward a small gatehouse flanking the warehouse doors.

I dart a terrified look at Captain Redfearn. What does that mean? Have we been exposed?

The security guard speaks to another in the gatehouse, and they both glance back at us.

My stomach drops. Redfearn's hands ball into fists at his sides.

Then the guard returns—with a manilla folder. The captain's license is dropped into it, the folder handed to Captain Redfearn. "Your charter," the guard says in gravelly, accented English, "Captain Malter."

There's a low, booming groan, and the monolithic doors begin to yawn aside. Captain Redfearn takes the folder in a daze.

The security guards part, and we enter Hibernacula.

The relief is so great, so overwhelming, that it takes me a moment to comprehend the sheer scale of what waits inside. The warehouse is as enormous as a hangar bay, dimly lit by lamps hanging between rows of boats stacked four tall on open racks like those outside. Another graveyard of them. Powerboats, cruisers, sportfishing yachts. But these boats are different—they're all cocooned in white or clear plastic shrink wrap, making me think of the white-draped furniture in Colding Mansion. As the hangar doors close behind us, a gust of wind blows through the warehouse, lofting and sucking the shrink wrap in and out in a crinkling sigh.

All the hairs on my arms stand on end.

"My God," Redfearn says, putting it together. His voice is hushed, as if we were in a church. Or a crypt. "*Hibernacula*," he whispers, the name breathy with revelation. "This is where they come to hibernate . . ."

I feel the cold on the back of my neck now.

"Normal flesh-and-blood yacht owners," Redfearn goes on, "they'll winter their boats because it's slow during the off-season." He waves a hand. "But these fucks winter their boats . . ."

"So they can sleep in them," I finish, my arms prickling now. "You mean . . . all of these are filled with the undead?"

We take in the rows upon rows of boats, like so many coffins, so many ghosts, shrink wrap gleaming in the gloom.

Captain Redfearn's throat bobs. "Let's find the *Thing* and get the fuck out of here."

Fine by me. We start pacing through the warehouse, looking for the bigger boats, when there's a shuddering groan—the doors opening again.

I take one look at the figure coming in after us, grab Captain Redfearn's hand and drag him behind me.

"What—" he starts.

"Shh!"

My heart is leap-frogging in my chest. I duck down the next aisle and push him against a fiberglass boat hull, stop his protestations with a finger to my lips. He stares at me, eyes wide in bewilderment, and I lean to whisper in his ear, "It's the captain Lair Yachting sent to hunt you."

Redfearn goes perfectly still.

We both wait, listening for the footfalls to fade, to tell us they're going in another direction.

But they're not. They're getting louder. Coming right for us.

I whirl, searching for a place to escape. To hide. The desperation of the burrowing animal rising in my veins.

Nowhere to go. We're trapped. These elevated boat hulls can't hide us entirely. We'll be spotted. They're going to find us and Redfearn will be recognized, and then—

Captain Redfearn finds the only answer.

He backs up to study the 50-foot cruiser we've been hiding behind, unzippers an access door that's been taped onto the plastic shrink wrap, steps aside and gestures.

I shake my head, my eyes pleading with him. *No. Please. Not in there.*

The footfalls are all but upon us. I can hear voices now.

Redfearn grabs my arm and shoves me up onto the stern and inside.

He dives in after me, zipping the door behind him as quietly as he can, wincing at the long rip of metal teeth coming together.

Then we're kneeling there in the dark womb of the boat, chests heaving, straining to hear.

It's cramped in here. Our bodies, in fact, our pressed against one another, and I am acutely aware of the captain's bicep brushing my breast. It's almost distracting enough to crowd out the terror pounding in me in this moment—and the footfalls that stop outside our boat.

I hold my breath.

A man speaks. "You have preference, Mr. Lelouch?" The voice is accented. Clearly Chinese.

The one that answers sounds African by way of French, if anything. Perhaps Algerian.

"As long as it's big," it grunts. "And fast."

There's a pause. "The *House of Shadows* should do. Ninety-four thousand horsepower. Can do thirty-two knots in deeper water."

"I'll take her."

"You have done this before?"

There's a footfall. I can see a shadow loom onto the shrink wrap before us. Then, a ferocious unzipping—

Captain Redfearn clamps a hand over my mouth to stop my scream.

But it's not our boat. It's another boat. A boat across from us. Another shadow out there, inspecting her. "Let's just say your employers' aversion to land has made me very . . . *useful*," that shadow says coolly. "As has been my experience working for my government, finding those who do not wish to be found." Another zipping sound; the inspection is complete. "So don't worry, friend. I'll find your Captain Redfearn."

Redfearn and I lock eyes, finding what is shared there, the same overwhelming emotion—fear. This is no shady yacht captain up for some extra cash. This guy is ex-military. This guy's a mercenary.

This guy's dangerous.

"And you think you'll find him here?" the Triad member scoffs, his tone dubious. "In Asia?"

There's a silence, as if a gaze has turned cold and hard. Then, "Redfearn was a gambler back in the day," Mr. Lelouch answers stonily. "The Chinese casinos were his favorites. And a guy fool enough to help his boss defy the Commodore?" There's a snort. "Naw, dude's got unfinished business with the vamps, I'd bet my life on it. And China has the highest concentration of them in the world." There's a grin in that voice now. "He'll turn up, one way or another. And I'll be waiting to cash in his chips when he does."

Footfalls again. I wait for them to fade, Redfearn's hand still clamped to my mouth, my eyes wandering now. There's something clinging to the inside of the shrink wrap. Condensation. I can feel it everywhere in here now. Smell it. The moisture. Something wrong.

I pull the captain's hand away. "Redfearn," I whisper.

"Shh," he says, distracted, trying to peer out through the plastic. "Just until we can't hear them anymore . . ."

But I'm not focused on that—I'm focused on what's behind us. This boat wasn't dried out before it was shrink wrapped and stored in here, and so whatever moisture present had been trapped inside. Leading to mildew. It mottles the interior, a black bloom covering the furnishings, the deck pillows, the back bench seat, a dark, creeping growth funneling toward the gaping door leading below . . .

My blood hammers in my ears.

And I hear it down there—*creeeek*—old wood groaning under the weight of something woken . . .

"Redfearn," I whisper, louder, sharp enough to wrench him around.

"What?"

And when I fancy seeing a shadow moving out of that darkness, trying to solidify into a shape, my heart is jumping into my throat and I'm pushing past Redfearn, my hands scrabbling for the zipper, racing it open, and I'm tumbling out and onto the concrete floor of the warehouse and scrambling backward, heaving dry sobs as Captain Redfearn follows me, zipping the access door shut behind him, his face white with alarm. "Hey," he says, hands outheld. "Hey, it's okay." But it's not okay. Because even as he kneels to hold me I can see, over his shoulder, a face pushing out against the white shrink wrap. Hollows stretching tight over the eyes and yawning mouth, fangs outlined, taloned hands reaching. And not the only face. Not the only boat. As I clutch to Redfearn and whirl about, it's all the boats. At the stern of each and every one lining the aisle on either side, faces are pushing against the shrink wrap, trying to break free like nightmares being born, tearing themselves out of surreal cauls, and the blood in my ears is the music of the world and the scar on my neck is throbbing like fire and I'm sobbing, "No, no, not again," and Captain Redfearn seeing my hand at my neck suddenly understands and buries me in his arms.

And then, all I hear is his voice.

"It's okay," he says. "It's not there. Do you hear me? It's just the PTSD. You've been traumatized." His voice, when I hear it again, is ragged with emotion. "You're okay. We'll both be okay."

And when I lift my head to look again, he's right. The faces are gone. Everything normal. No nightmares pushing against the boat covers.

Just us.

"Maybe," Redfearn says, his voice growing deeper, regretful. "Maybe this was a mistake—"

"What? No," I say, wiping at my eyes so I can look at him. "Don't say that. "

His stubbled face is twisted with guilt, his eyes glassy. "I shouldn't have brought you with me—"

But I shake my head, push myself to my feet and smooth my hair into place. "Don't be ridiculous. I'm fine."

He stands too, sighing. "Mrs. Colding—"

But I turn away. "We should find the boat," I say, sniffing. "Before our friend comes back."

He scowls, unable to argue with that.

It's down the next aisle that we find the big boats. Only a few of them crowding the gleaming main floor, resting on chocks and transport chassis. Redfearn seems to sense the right one immediately. He climbs a ladder onto the aft of a medium-sized superyacht. Its top half is shrink wrapped, the cover snugged down to right above the rub rail encircling the boat. He grabs the bottom of the wrap and pulls up, revealing tall stainless-steel letters: *THING*.

He turns to me and grins.

It's that grin I've always loved—a little rakish, a little dangerous. It makes me want to prove something to him. Because now that the rush of adrenaline has passed, a creeping embarrassment is overtaking me. Before I know it, I'm approaching a tender boat that's been tucked under the *Thing*'s hull. I don't know what I'm looking for, but I find it. An excuse for a conversation. To make up for my uncharacteristic moment of vulnerability. "She seems to be quite the entertainment boat."

Captain Redfearn hops down to see what I'm talking about. He lifts it out of the tender's stern and stands it in front of him—a striped foam surfboard. A wistful smile breaks across his face. "Now that takes me back."

I shoot him an incredulous glance. "You used to surf?"

He arches a brow. "Am I that dull?"

I arch a brow back.

He gives me a dirty, half-lidded look and turns back to the board, runs a marveling hand down its length. "Believe it or not, I used to surf with the boys when I was in the Navy. We were always on the water. Wasn't a whole lot else to do."

I cross my arms, eyes narrowed, imagining Captain Redfearn young and shirtless and crouching under the rippling curl of a wave. The image makes me tingle. "I still can't see it."

His mouth crooks as he brushes grit off the board. "Suit yourself."

I humph, arms crossing tighter. "Then you'll have to prove it to me."

This gets me a surprised, sidelong look. "You're going to surf with me?"

"Not on that," I concede, and pull something else out of the tender. "But I can on this."

When he sees the electric hydrofoil board, his face falls. "No . . ."

I smirk. "*Yes.*"

"That's not true surfing . . ."

"Oh, hush," I say, waving a hand in dismissal. "You need to start doing things that make you uncomfortable. Besides working for bloodthirsty monsters, that is." When he still hesitates, I give him a look. "For me?"

And he looks at me under the swoop of the *Thing*'s hull in Hibernacula, trying with all his might to be grumpy and completely failing, his eyes sparkling.

TEN

CAPTAIN REDFEARN

"Where are we going?" I grumble-shout into Mrs. Colding's ear.

She smiles at my question. She stands at the helm of the RIB, fine wisps of hair escaping from her bun and whipping behind her in the wind as she turns to look at me. Her face is alight with something fierce and free that I do not want to question. "You'll see."

We've taken two efoil boards with us, stashing them in the stern. It's late night now, and I have no clue where we are. Somewhere off mainland China. All I can see is dark sky and stars, tumbled silhouettes of green mountains along the coast. I don't know what she has planned. I only know she's trying to prove something. That she's still up for this, not affected by this violence. The sweetness of it makes my heart ache.

But what if I'm not good for her? What if that mercenary was not just a threat returning, but a shadow from the past, promising a return to it?

What if I only bring that violence back into her life?

What if I am the violence?

When the boat slaps across a particularly large swell, making me glance behind, I grasp what's in store for us. The sight draws me to the stern, lips parted as I stare, my face bathed in light. The water frothing behind the twin propellers looks like a slipstream of bluish and gray smoke glittering with stars. It's a wake of constellations laid out on the sea, a liquid aurora borealis sparkling as if with cobalt fireflies—a wonder of bioluminescent plankton. It is strange and enchanting and eerily beautiful.

"My father took me here when I was little," Mrs. Colding calls back to me. "There are few places like this. It has always been my secret." She cuts the engine, tosses the anchor over the side and turns to face me. I can't help but stare. We'd found swimsuits in the yacht, tags still hanging on them, no doubt leftovers from some guest's shopping spree. I made do with board shorts printed in a tropical splash of palm trees. The black one-piece she found, however, is magnificent. It is very her—both bewitching and sophisticated, with a plunging neckline and contoured shape that shows off all those curves I've been dying to see for years now. I feel a dangerous stirring in my shorts. Fuck me, it's almost a crime for her to look that good at her age. But it's precisely her age that makes her look so good. Because there is nothing so beautiful as a woman who has been sculpted by all the joys and trials and heartbreaks of life, and who has been left fierce-boned and glowing, uniquely her. Uniquely Mrs. Colding.

The boat rocks on the sea, and I find that we've been staring at each other for a long time.

There's a small smile on her lips, but her voice is very serious. "Redfearn?"

I snap out of it, feeling the heat rushing to my cheeks, and haul up one of the efoil boards with a sigh. "If we're doing this, you're gonna have to teach me."

Minutes later, we're both in the water with helmets and life jackets on, blue light glowing about us as we tread water and grip our boards. They're Fliteboards—basically paddleboards with short masts hanging underwater with carbon stabilizing wings and an electric motor attached at the end. But damn if it isn't hard to mount the thing.

"Just wait," Mrs. Colding says, trying not to laugh as I flop onto the board. "You need to take your time. Let's start slow, okay? We'll start at level four. Now hold down the trigger on the controller." I blink at the black plastic remote in my hand, squeeze the trigger. There's an electric whine and I feel a flurry of water beneath me. Our boards surge forward in a froth of glowy bioluminescence and I grip onto my latches, cursing.

Mrs. Colding fights back a smile. "You okay?"

I grimace for her. "Perfect."

"I'll show you how to stand, all right? You get onto your knees first." She slowly slides her knees up until she's kneeling on the board, back straight and chest out, and goddamn it's hard not to look at how her ass sticks out in that pose. The nose of her Fliteboard lifts off the waves and she adjusts her weight, bringing it back down. "When you've got the hang of it," she says, "you can increase the speed and try standing. I'll go first." She taps on her controller and I hear the pitch of her motor's whine rise. She begins to pull away from me, leaving turbulent light behind her. I see her wobble a moment, and when she straightens out, she brings her left foot in front of her and slowly stands into a lunge position, sliding her weight back so that the board rises out of the water on its mast and she's gliding above the waves. It's smooth as hell.

She glances back at me with a grin. "Your turn."

"Right," I grumble. "Easy-peasy."

Mrs. Colding leans her body slightly to circle back so she can watch. I slide up onto my knees, feeling the board judder under me, bouncing up and down on the chop.

"Increase your speed just a little," Mrs. Colding calls.

I tap my controller and the bouncing stops, the board settling into a steady cruise. Mrs. Colding nods. "Feel good?"

I give her a thumbs up.

"Try standing. Increase the speed and take it slow. If you fall, jump away from the foil so you don't get cut up."

"Why do I feel like one of your stewardesses right now?" I grouse.

She fails in suppressing a smirk. "Having trouble taking orders, captain?"

I give her a look, then tap my controller. The efoil surges much faster than I'd like. Spray mists my face. This is nothing like surfing; the balancing is all different. But standing should be the same. Planting my hands in front of me, I scooch one foot forward and rise, hands out, wobbling, toes gripping the foam deck grip.

"That's it," Mrs. Colding calls. "You got it, you got—"

I don't got it. Suddenly, I feel the efoil lurch sickeningly out from under me and I'm eating seawater, the efoil rocketing up out of the waves like a bathtub toy bobbing to the surface. When I come up, blowing water and pinching it from my eyes, I see Mrs. Colding trying to keep from falling off her Fliteboard from laughing.

"All right, all right," I grumble, splashing water her way and stroking toward my disgraced efoil. "I see what you're doing. You did this to humiliate me, didn't you?"

"I'm sorry," Mrs. Colding says, holding her stomach. "I'm sorry. I just—that was the funniest—"

I smirk. It's hard, it is very hard not to when she's laughing like that. I don't think I've seen her laugh so hard, or so freely. Already, I am certain, it is my favorite sound in the world.

"Come on, old surfer," she calls, a smile in her voice. "I believe in you."

"Fucking efoil boards," I grumble. I grab mine and haul myself onto it, tap my controller so I'm up to speed again. When I've slid up onto my knees, Mrs. Colding curves about so she's keeping pace with me, her mast sinking back down into the water so she's bumping along as I am.

"Ready?" she says.

When I look up at her, there is no mirth in her face. She is the most serious I have ever seen her.

I nod.

"Come on."

I look ahead, jaw clenching, and tap my controller. The motor whines again. The board surges forward across the waves. When I slide my foot forward and stand, I make sure my weight isn't as far back this time. The board wavers, but does not slide away. I test shifting my weight, bringing the nose up and down. It's solid beneath me. I am in control. A small, disbelieving smile tugs at my mouth.

Mrs. Colding watches me with a strange expression in her eyes. "Ready to fly?"

Another nod.

"Let's go faster first." We both tap our controllers and our boards race across the water, the bow waves kicking up the noses of our boards. "Push down hard with your front foot," Mrs. Colding orders. I do, modeling her, and my board planes and flattens off. "More speed now." We tap at our controllers, bringing up our speed to an almost frightening pace. We must be doing twenty-five kilometers per hour. The water whips by below, roiling with blue light, and I feel the beginning of some nameless joy rise up within me. Mrs. Colding senses it. She looks over at me, eyes shining. "Takeoff time." She shifts her weight back again, and I follow suit. We are in rhythm, in intimate synchronicity.

Then I feel it.

Our boards rise. The noise changes as they leave the water, dripping droplets as they glide up into the air in a precarious sense of flight, an ascent that is both exhilarating and terrifying. A giddiness takes me, and I can't help it—I let out a triumphant bark of laughter.

Mrs. Colding watches me with shining eyes. I know, with utter certainty, that she has just taught me something I cannot name.

Then she leans away and peels off, carving like a snowboarder through fresh powder. I follow, almost willing my board after her. Before long, we are tracing trails of brilliant blue algae across the sea together, turning it into a churning glory of light. Without a word, without planning it, we weave in and out of each other's paths, natural as breathing. This is not surfing. This is not even flying. This is a dance.

This is courtship.

As we glide up alongside each other, we find we're not alone. All around us, ghostly bluish forms are gliding up from the deeps, like guides leading us to the spirit world. A pod of them with glowing outlines, fins and flippers trailing streamers of white light: dolphins. They dive in and out of the water in sparkling splashes, cavorting about us like a benediction, a blessing. Mrs. Colding laughs in delight and turns to me, as unguardedly and dazzlingly happy as I've ever seen her, and something strange clutches at my heart. *What has happened to us?* I wonder. *Where are we? Where have we come to?* Something almost like sorrow rolls through me, squeezing my throat shut. There is not even room for time in this moment. Time seems to have stopped altogether.

Until Mrs. Colding nosedives into the water.

"Mrs. Colding!" The shock grips me for a split second, harrowing and absolute. Then I'm leaping off my efoil and plunging into the water after her, tucking my controller into my life jacket so I can stroke toward her with my hands free. She's not moving. Did her efoil cut her? Did the propeller—did it—is she—

But when I drag her life jacket around, she's just holding her head, a shiny chip in her helmet. "Sorry," she says. "Just hit my—"

But I've already stopped her by crushing her to me.

We both remember in the same instant. Her body stiffens with self-consciousness, and when I let go she pulls back enough so she can look up at me from under her lashes, her eyes uncertain, searching. I can feel her breath on my face, still feel the touch of her body. The intimacy of it makes my dick twitch in my shorts.

This is definitely not waiting.

"Well," she says, her hands slowly sliding down my shoulders, dropping away. She chances a look into my eyes again before dropping hers and shuddering. "We should probably—"

"No."

She meets my eyes again, her brows crinkled in a question. So I make my way toward an answer.

"We're being stupid," I announce.

The corner of her mouth twitches. "Are we?"

"Yes." I take one of her hands, and we both look down at that intertwining of fingers as we bob there in the ocean, creating swirls of bioluminescence around us. I can hear her holding her breath. We're inches apart. "There's no avoiding this, is there?" I say, and it's surprisingly hard to keep my voice steady. I swallow and try again. "There's no . . . getting around this attraction while we're doing this."

She's very carefully still watching our hands. "So what are you saying?"

"Maybe," I say, and shrug. "Maybe we could agree to take it slow?"

She looks up at me again. She's fighting hard to not let her lips twist into a smirk. But she can't hide what's in her eyes—they're dancing. "And I thought you were going to be stupid forever, Captain Redfearn," she says.

I can't help but laugh as she watches me, her eyes alight.

It's almost enough to dispel the feeling that I've made a mistake.

CAPTAIN'S LOG

Hibernacula to Hong Kong, December 9th.

Ship: *Thing*.

Speed: 15 knots.

Distance: 16 mi.

Weather: Calm night.

Notes: *Thing* is provisioned. Inspected her yesterday, bow to stern. Hull and controls. Engine and fuel. Electrical and safety equipment. Cabins and features. Mrs. Colding was right—she's built for entertainment. Plenty of toys, hot tubs, pools and beach clubs. Seems to be all glass, made for housing light. But there's also something of the freighter about her. A cold and unfeeling means of transportation. And a hint at what she carries with an anti-piracy sound cannon at the bow.

I leave the interior to Mrs. Colding.

Yesterday crew arrived. All Chinese. Went to work cleaning boat for next charter without a word, Mrs. Colding directing them.

I did not think of shadows of the past. Or what may be waiting for us.

Checked charter packet. A yacht controller on a lanyard slid out first—haven't used one of those before. Followed by yacht documents and chart of South China Sea with a dot circled in red some miles off coast from Macau: **21°44'06.2"N 113°31'29.7"E**. My destination.

The last sheet of paper detailed charter itself. A single sentence: **Pick up passengers on December 9th at 0000 at Hong Kong Marina, Pier 9 and transport to destination**.

It is 0000 hours now.

ELEVEN

MRS. COLDING

I turn our date over and over in my mind as I get the *Thing* ready.

It is an obsession, as compulsive as my need to clean, to scour and scrub until all things have revealed their true selves to me. Yes, the relief of being back on a yacht again is overwhelming. I slip into my old role as chief stew as easily as breathing, feeling purposeful and surefooted now that I have my sea legs again. But all that is eclipsed by my need to parse that night with Captain Redfearn down to the finest detail.

As I order the taciturn stews to hoover and microclean grout from floor tiles with toothpicks, I try to interpret every look, every touch, every moment of that night. The way he looked, shirtless, in those board shorts still brings a faint blush to my cheeks. As does the way he looked at me in my swimsuit after I threw the anchor overboard, making me feel like the sexiest woman alive. I think of the way we locked eyes as we glided across those neon currents of bioluminescence, the way I seemed to fill his world. Goose bumps shiver my arms as I think back on it.

What had he been thinking then? Had he been thinking what I thought? Had he thought that time had stopped?

Had he thought, *This is magic?*

I jerk myself out of this, old cautions reasserting themselves as I scrub a gold-plated sink clean. Am I ready, after all this time? Am I ready to open myself up to hurt again? Am I ready to trust again?

And there is that disquieting flicker of doubt. What did Redfearn do to that captain to get his license? What violence was he capable of?

Still. These new feelings course through me, threatening a dangerous mushiness. I can't help thinking of the way he looked as we bobbed there in all that elusive, enchanting light, water droplets clinging to his stubble and silver brows, his gray eyes glowing blue with reflected bioluminescence and a burning need for me. I can't help thinking how badly I'd wanted him to kiss me in that moment.

Best to distract myself.

I tour the *Thing*'s interior for a final inspection before we pick up the guests. She's a stunning boat, if a bit hollow-feeling. Maybe it has to do with all her glass features welcoming in the light, making her look like a piece of floating glass architecture. There are her full-length windows in all the suites. A glass elevator traveling through all the decks, roofed with a skylight and enveloped by a floating spiral staircase also composed of glass. It opens up on an airy glass pavilion on top of the boat that affords guests ocean views in every direction.

And at the bottom of the elevator shaft, I step out into the lower deck saloon with its cream-colored teak decking and rows of portholes. Light wavers everywhere here in surreal patterns, its peacefulness almost suspect, and I look up. Where the ceiling should be is a long rectangle of glass containing twenty-five thousand gallons of water: a glass-bottomed infinity pool on the main deck. That should be a hit with the guests.

The saloon, the lounges, the pavilion, the suites—all clean, all ready. No excuses left.

I can feel okay giving in now and rewarding myself with his presence.

I find him at the bow. He's practicing with that yacht controller he found in the charter packet he received on Hibernacula. Its yellow lanyard hangs around his neck as his fingers clumsily maneuver the controls, and I bite back a smile as he curses under his breath and pilots us around a ferry traversing Hong Kong's busy harbor. He's wearing dress whites, as is custom for receiving guests, his white polo decorated with a captain's epaulettes. He looks devilishly handsome.

"Getting the hang of it?" I ask as I join him at the rail.

His scowl unravels a bit at one corner. He grunts. "That's a generous way of putting it."

I grip the rail with both hands to steady myself, taking in a shivery breath. I'm almost trembling with nerves, with infuriating gooeyness. We haven't spoken of last night yet, and the need to comment on it, to touch that magic again as if to make it real, to reassure me that it happened and wasn't some fantastical dream, is overpowering. "So," I say in my best teasing voice. "Did last night change your mind about efoil boards?"

He can't stop his scowl from unraveling all the way now, and I revel in a silly feeling of victory. "It's still not true surfing."

"No," I say, shrugging one shoulder, and give him a sidelong look. "But I'm sure we can agree it has its perks."

He chuckles now, warm and deep, and that feeling of victory washes over me like champagne, deliciously addictive. "This is true," he says.

"Shall we surf again soon?"

"Now, I wouldn't go *that* far," he says, making me laugh now. Then he turns to me, more serious. "But I'd like to spend time with you soon, after we pick up the guests. If you'd like that."

It's almost too much, him looking at me like that. I have to try very hard to not flutter my eyes away. "Yes," I say, hushed, feeling like a girl as heat rushes up my neck. "Yes, I'd like that."

There's a deep rumble of amusement in his voice. "Good," he says, satisfied, and turns to sweep the approaching marina with his gray eyes. "We're almost there. Just have to get these passengers squared away and—"

But then everything in his face changes, and my heart drops as I turn to look, too. There's a gaggle of Asian beauties waiting on the concrete pier floating toward us. They wave and shriek with laughter, hopping up and down in their excitement as they call out in English and Mandarin. "Hello! Nî hâo!" Their lovely young faces shine, sparkly phones gripped in their hands, handbags on their shoulders, legs long and bare and shapely in stilettos. Out of the ten of them, none look older than twenty-one.

Dread slides like a rock down from my throat, into my chest, lodging like a cannonball in my gut.

Captain Redfearn and I look at each other.

The *Thing* glides up alongside the pier, and in moments the passengers are boarding. They shuffle shy and barefoot across the passerelle with heels dangling from fingertips, bowing their heads to Captain Redfearn and I, whispering and pointing as they gape about at the yacht with awed faces. They look like orphans. Runaways. Lost children who believe they've gotten their big break in life.

If only they knew why they were truly chosen.

I should have known. I don't know what I thought. If I had for more than a second, I would have put it together—the only possible reason passengers would be transported to the Commodore's base.

And as they pass, they all dump their phones into my hands, until there's so many of them I have to stuff them into the pockets of my skirt. Yes. That makes sense. That would be in their contract. No pictures are allowed on yachts, usually, to preserve the privacy of the owners. But the Steward wouldn't want any way for these girls to communicate with the outside world once what happens to them begins to happen.

When I turn to Captain Redfearn again, all the color has left his face. "What are we going to do?" I whisper.

He opens his mouth to answer, but at that moment a shadow drifts to the end of the passerelle. It had been waiting there with the girls all along.

Their handler.

It's a man. Chinese, narrow as a blade, eyes hidden behind black sunglasses. He's dressed all in black and has his hands clasped behind him. He looks like a mortician.

Captain Redfearn swallows, glances at me. "Stay here." I open my mouth to argue, but one look at that figure on the pier and my body warns, *Stay*.

Redfearn descends the passerelle slowly. He does not fully disembark, choosing instead to stop at the gangplank's end, not stepping foot on the pier. A boundary.

His back is stiff. His tone stiffer. "Yes?"

The sunglasses gleam at him. An envelope is held out.

Captain Redfearn looks down at it, takes it. When he looks up again, the man has melted away into the shadows of the pier.

I let out a breath I didn't know I was holding, unroot myself and come down to Redfearn so I'm looking over his shoulder. "What is it?"

His head is bowed. He's opened the envelope and is reading a note written in a spidery hand. His voice comes out distant, distracted. "It's the Steward. He wants me to pick up another passenger and bring him with us."

Something presses against my lungs. "Pick him up where?"

Captain Redfearn holds up a hand, still reading, and now I see the other thing that was in the envelope, lying in his open palm like a dollop of blood: a red poker chip, the kind you'd see at a casino. I pluck it out of the rough folds of Redfearn's hand, and when I turn it between my fingers the light catches it, picking out the pair of gold eyeteeth stamped on its face, the gilt lettering rimming its edge.

It reads *Palace of the Fang*.

TO CAPTAIN MALTER

My apologies for a last-minute addition to your passenger list. My ever-troublesome blood son, Pongshu, is in somewhat of a bind. He possesses a regrettable gambling habit, which seems to have led him to losing his yacht at poker. He is stranded on *The Palace of the Fang*, and I would consider it a courtesy if you fetched him for me before he gets himself into any more trouble. I think it high time he found himself disciplined.

It will be a detour for you, but one I hope proves valuable. I am sure you will see more of my blood son during your employment with me, and you may as well start learning how to handle him now.

Do exercise caution. He's a slippery fellow, and rather bity when drunk.

Looking forward to our introduction with great interest,

The Steward

CAPTAIN'S LOG

Hong Kong to *The Palace of the Fang*, December 9th.
Ship: *Thing*.
Speed: 25 knots.
Distance: 40 mi.
Weather: Clear night.
Notes: Fuck.

TWELVE
CAPTAIN REDFEARN

I stand at the bow tugging uneasily at the choking bowtie of my black gala tux, cheeks still stinging from a fresh shave, and study the faded blue nautical chart in my hands. It's from the sheaf of charts I'd saved up over my years as captain of the *Lair*, one of the few belongings I took with me on this trip. This one's a closeup of the southern coast of China. There's Macau with its opulent offerings. And not far down the shoreline, where it turns to rugged cliffs, a small red "X" I'd made years ago when I'd learned the coordinates from Adrian. My chicken scratch beneath: *The Palace of the Fang*.

I had heard about it for years. Hard not to. Its reputation, dark and glamorous and sparkling with danger, tendrilled through the Lairverse like a seductive poison. But I had never seen it. I had made sure of that.

And now I had no choice but to walk through its doors.

As I'm rolling up the chart, there's a footstep behind me. I turn, expecting Mrs. Colding, but it's one of the guests. Her friends had disappeared below deck some time ago, babbling excitedly. Mrs. Colding had led them, her chilly stewardess demeanor firmly back in place, and

I had smiled to see all the models hush around her. This girl is not so easily cowed, though—the jut of her chin speaks to a certain boldness that's still a little rough around the edges, that hasn't yet learned its place. We stand in comfortable silence a moment before I speak.

"Why aren't you with your friends?"

She slides a thread of silky black hair out of her eyes. "Too restless."

"Must've been a big day for you."

She looks about at the yacht glowing like a spaceship in the night. "I never . . ." She waves a hand. "I come from small village. This change everything." She looks down at her clothes, a tight top and bubblegum skirt that's so mini it's practically a belt. "These not even mine. They bought these for me."

I tap the rolled-up chart into one hand, feeling a hard discomfort twist at my insides. Is that what Penelope was offered? Is this how they won her over?

"And what do they want in return?" I ask, a little stiffly.

She shrugs a small shoulder, her eyes on the sea. "What men always want."

The matter-of-fact tone in which she says it, the offhandedness that's too weary to even be cynicism, brings on an immense sadness. "What's your name?"

She looks me up and down, a wariness entering her face. "Bing."

"Bing." I draw a measured breath. Then say, harder than I mean to, "Maybe it's not worth it, Bing."

She gives me a long look with her dark, heavy-lidded eyes. "You not woman. You know nothing." She blinks up at the glass pavilion on top of the boat, releasing me. "Hot tub up there?"

I nod and she pads away in her bare feet, more than ready to take this new world for all it's worth.

I'm still staring after her when Mrs. Colding drifts up to me.

She lifts a delicate brow when she sees my tux, one side of her mouth twitching, but holds her tongue for now. "They're all settled in." She follows my gaze, watching Bing climb the stairs to the sun deck. "We need to get them off the boat before we arrive at the Commodore's base."

"I know," I grumble, and loft the chart for *The Palace of the Fang* before tucking it into a breast pocket. "But I need to take care of this first."

This brings her attention back to my fitted black tux. She openly admires it, a small smile curling her lips as she steps up to me and smooths my shoulders, the sweeping breadth of my chest under the tuxedo jacket. Then her eyes lift, twinkling, to my bare cheeks, my hair slicked back in a silver wave. "Look at you," she marvels in a low, smoky voice that makes my insides go funny. "All cleaned up. This place must be something if it can get you clean-shaven and in a suit."

I try for a smile, but it dies on my lips. She chucks up my chin. "Hey." She catches my eyes. "You going to tell me about this *Palace of the Fang*?"

I return her look, my eyes moving back and forth between hers. Should I tell her what I'm dreading now? Doesn't she know already?

In the end, I don't get the chance to reply—the first mate's voice crackles to life from the crew radio tucked into my pocket. "We're here, Captain."

And, suddenly, we are. We round a bend along the coastline and a sparkling bay opens before us. It's filled with a scattering of superyachts tied to mooring buoys, their lights shivering on the water. They're all assembled like devotees before a granite cliff face, its top fringed in a dangling bramble of green vines. But what have they gathered for?

Very faint, two pinpricks of orange light flicker in the cliff face.

There.

I pull the crew radio out of my pocket and bring it to my lips. "All right, I'm taking over." Next, I pull out the yacht controller, hold down the dual power buttons and wait for its lights to flash solid yellow, indicating the boat's control has transferred to me. Then I glide the *Thing* forward with the joystick, maneuvering her around the other yachts floating in the bay. As we pass, figures appear on those other decks to watch us, their gazes raising goosepimples on my skin. But before long we've moved beyond the grouped yachts and there's only a stretch of dark water between us and a sheer wall of gray rock, ancient and pitted by time and wind and sea spray—and something else.

There's a tall, narrow crack in that cliff face, yawning upward in a scream, and those pinpricks of light are a pair of braziers set into holes in the rock above, blazing like fiery eyes.

A tunnel.

"What is this place?" Mrs. Colding breathes, those braziers reflected in twin crazes of flame in her pupils.

I swallow hard in a dry throat. "It's their casino."

Mrs. Colding lets out a harsh snort. "What have they to gamble for? They have everything!"

I edge her a look. "What else would their kind gamble for?"

The color goes out of her high cheeks and she turns to look back at the tunnel. "So I'm not going with you, then."

I shake my head, slowly, left to right.

She takes a moment to process this. Then she sees me staring at my palm, and what's trembling in it—the poker chip from *The Palace of the Fang.* A sad sympathy gentles her features. With her eyes on mine, slowly, very slowly, she lays delicate fingers on my wrist. "You going to be okay in there?"

I feel a scary urge to bark laughter. I wish I knew.

But I do not say that out loud. Instead, I close my hand over the chip, slip it into my pocket and flash her a croupier's cocky smile. "I'll be in and out before you know it."

Mrs. Colding eyes me, the bay of white boats. "The whole Nosferyachtu Club is out for your head, and you're going straight into their den. If you're spotted—"

"It's a chance I'll have to take."

She shakes her head, nostrils flaring. "I don't like this."

"I know." I press the speaker button on my crew radio. "Bring the tender around."

Mrs. Colding follows me to the swim deck. She looks lost, her pale face numb, as if she were caught in a dream that's getting away from her, a calamitous and incomprehensible turn of events. When the deckhands bring the tender alongside and I hand the crew radio and yacht controller to the first mate, this final act of preparation seems to snap her out of her trance. She darts forward and grabs my arm. "This is a bad—"

I don't let her finish. I grab the back of her head with one hand and pull her into a deep, bruising kiss, putting all my fierce love into it, telling her with my mouth: *You are everything to me, and I am coming back to you.*

When I pull away, she stares at me, breathless, swollen lips parted, her face white with shock. Message understood.

Then I'm pressing my lips to her knuckles, easing myself backward into the tender as I do. "I'll see you soon," I promise and give her my best roguish smile, pouring all my confidence into it, trying to convince us both. And then I'm casting off and droning the tender away toward the tunnel and *The Palace of the Fang*, Mrs. Colding watching after me with one hand to her stomach, looking like a ghost.

THIRTEEN
MRS. COLDING

When the tender drones up to the tunnel in that bare cliff face, I can't watch anymore. I can't bear to see it—see him—be swallowed by that darkness. I wrench away into the interior of the *Thing*, groping through companionways until I'm in my suite. I pace in circles, wringing my hands and letting out little wheezing noises of fury and complaint, unable to stop thinking of it. It blocks up my entire world with its presence, making the air heavy: his kiss. That kiss I'd been waiting for, longing for, and now he's given it to me and it was as beautiful and heart-wrenching as a curse. *You have cursed me, Captain Redfearn. You have cursed me with your love.* My hands are trembling, one thumb working repetitively, feverishly into another palm as that familiar need clutches me, rocketing through the gray folds of my brain like a virus, demanding gratification: Clean. I have to clean. I whirl about, searching for something, anything, to make fresh and new, to distract myself from what is happening. I scrabble through the ensuite head, slap on yellow latex gloves and grab a scrub brush, scour already sparkling tiles on all fours as if I can scour away the images in my head, the image of Captain Redfearn sailing away from me, the image of him lying in a pool of blood, the image of our love drained away and gone forever. Clean.

FOURTEEN
CAPTAIN REDFEARN

Fifty feet from the tunnel, I look over my shoulder for a last glimpse of Mrs. Colding's form on the swim deck, but it's not there. She's gone.

I push away a small twinge of disappointment. I understand. I wouldn't want her to watch, either. I wouldn't want her to have to watch this.

Clamping my jaw, I turn back to face the tunnel.

It's even bigger up close, a throat of gaping darkness. I can see water foaming inside it, surging in leaps of white spray against a small boulder jutting out of the sea to the right of the entrance. I blink to make sure I'm seeing correctly. There's a man hunkered on that boulder. Barefooted. Stick-limbed. In a black traditional jacket with a row of frog buttons down its front, looking like a relic from the dynasties of ancient China.

When the brim of the man's straw cone hat lifts, two pinpricks of cold light glow out of a sunken face.

"Fare," the figure rasps, holding out a withered hand, its nails curled into yellowing talons.

For a boat is there, rocking in the swells behind the boulder, two Chinese lanterns hanging from poles at its front. I know what that is. It's a flat-bottomed sampan of black wood, its lacquer long faded. Just narrow enough to fit into the tunnel, unlike my modern tender.

So that's how it works here.

I kill the engine and let the tender coast to the boulder, balance one foot on my bobbing foredeck and precariously lean to pass my poker chip to the boatman.

The boatman holds the chip up to the light and inspects it, wipes a thumb across the gold teeth inlay. "Name?"

"Captain Malter. Of the *Thing*."

The cold pinpricks under the brim scrutinize me. A thin lip retracts to reveal two long, yellow fangs.

Then the chip vanishes inside that rag of a jacket and a clawed hand beckons.

I toss the bowline to him. As he ties it off around a knob of rock, I hop onto the boulder and board his little sampan. It rocks dangerously a moment, but the boatman is as quick and agile as a wharf rat. He seats himself in the stern and pulls the cord on an old outboard motor. It coughs to life and the lanterns on their poles rock and sway as the sampan swings about. The idea of turning my back on this wretch gives me the creeps, but I can't help myself—I can't keep my eyes off that tunnel. Nothing for it, then, but to stand at the bow, feet planted wide for balance and one hand in the pocket of my immaculate tux, so I can watch it approach.

A cool skein of unease is winding about my spine. I've been to many places in the Lairverse, but there is something artificial about the presentation here, a theatrical staginess that unsettles. The braziers blazing in their alcoves look like eyes more than ever. And now that I'm closer, close enough to see the rock glistens, slick with sea mist, I notice there are stalactites hanging like fangs from the roof of the tunnel entrance, giving it the air of some haunted theme park attraction. It is a yawning fiend's mouth, waiting to swallow me whole. Those stone teeth pass overhead, and my heart jumps against my breastbone as a wave of darkness falls on me. I feel as if I am a child again, as if I have been yanked back to a time when I could be transported by both terror and wonder. This is a game. I am passing through the entrance to some spooky tunnel of love at a country fair.

But there's no love waiting in that tunnel, or on the other side of it.

Just darkness. The scraping of the boat against the narrow walls. And the eyes. The eyes of the things lining the tunnel roof, filmy black wings enshrouding themselves. The eyes of the bats looking down at me, glittering red in the faint glow of the sampan's lanterns.

The hairs on my arms stand on end.

The fears are coming. The fear of what I am walking into. I am gripped by the grim certainty that whatever pulsing hell of temptation lies beyond this tunnel, whatever I'm about to see, has been waiting for me all my life.

And then I am passing out of the far end of the tunnel, and everything is light.

My lips part in stupid awe. The sampan has glided out into an open cave shaped like a colosseum. Rippling stone walls soar hundreds of feet into the night, enclosing a private lake. And on that lake floats *The Palace of the Fang*.

It is a festival of light. A ferry or barge that's been converted into a glitzy, three-story floating casino built in the imperial style of a Chinese palace, glowing as lurid and fantastical as a fairy tale. Its curved roofs and red gables gleam, illuminated by neon lights, torches, braziers. And floating on the surface of the water about it—hundreds of paper lanterns flickering like votive candles. Just when I think there can't be any more light, there's a pop and fizzing crackle, and fireworks explode into the night sky above the palace's horned towers, turning the lake into shimmering fire. A hidden world of luxury. A vision.

A trap.

I feel a tug on my elbow and look down to see the boatman's hand pulling away. My skin goes strange. That can't be right. Because the boatman sits in the stern, a good six feet from me. His head hunches down between his bony shoulders as he shows his teeth in a ratty little smile. "One must heed the rules," he rasps. "No blood spilled on palace grounds." A talon points skyward. "The ones who sleep above will pass judgment."

I crane my neck to look, and that's when I see the coffins.

The fireworks reveal them in startling flashes, shadows leaping long: They're all about the inside of the open-roofed cave. Hundreds of them, of every make and period. And they hang—precariously, bizarrely, impossibly—on beams jutting out of the cliff walls. Old pine boxes. Caskets lampblacked and slaked in lime. Sarcophagi scrawled with vermilion calligraphy. Hollowed-out tree trunks from forests long dead. Rows and rows of them, spiraling all the way up to the shadowy heights of the cave walls like some airy necropolis. A sky graveyard. A colony of the damned. Some leaning, pitching drunkenly. Others so ancient they're falling apart, mottled white with bird droppings. The lids of a few creak up, and the following burst of fireworks ignites the cinders of many pairs of eyes watching me.

My flesh goes cold all over my body.

The mournful chug of the motor lets me know it's been killed, and I see that we're coasting up to the casino's jetty. With a spry hop I'm aboard and gazing about at the palace strung with lights, its landing stage for the reception of the bored undead. There are other sampans with their little lanterns here, other boatmen waiting. And before me, up a flight of steps flanked by roaring braziers and the statues of lions, the doorway to *The Palace of the Fang*. Rounded, adorned in a hallucinatory ornateness of design that evokes an enmeshment of teeth, of fangs.

Because there are fangs. The double doors bristle with them. There must be thousands of teeth studding them, their roots embedded deep in the wood around that design in the center, tips projecting outward as if in defense of what lies within. A barbaric and somehow majestic sight.

I can feel a muscle twitch at the corner of my eye. I can still feel Mrs. Colding's lips on mine, burning like fire, as hot as the danger and temptation that waits beyond those doors, ready to show me what I am. What I fear I am.

What I always have been.

My nails bite into my palms, hard and angry, and I realize, for the first time in a long time, that I'm afraid.

As a Navy SEAL, I had never known fear. There had been too much anger for there to be any room left over for fear. I had thrown myself into it, content to gamble with my life as recklessly as my money. Because I never had anything to lose before.

But now I do. Now I have Penelope. Now I have Mrs. Colding.

Now is when I can't afford to be a gambler anymore.

Fireworks explode, the glow of those sparkling flowers bathing my face, and I think, *For you, Pen. This is for you.*

This is for my little sun.

"Heed the rules," the boatman repeats behind me, a sly note in his voice that I do not like. Then I'm filling my chest with a long, steadying breath, eyes very carefully avoiding those coffins hanging in the fitful glare above. And I'm moving. I'm striding up those steps and the bodyguards are opening the double doors for me, ungrinning that gnashing of teeth to usher me inside, into a world of glamour and terror and darkness.

FIFTEEN
MRS. COLDING

When I wipe the sweat from my brow and sit back, the bristles of the scrub brush are crazed or worn down to the handle, my fingers throbbing and threatening blisters.

Everything clean. Every one of my troubles still there.

I toss the scrub brush aside and climb to my feet, walk out of the ensuite head. I need to be out on deck, in case he needs me. In case . . . in case . . .

But I can't think about that.

SIXTEEN
CAPTAIN REDFEARN

The first vampire I see inside is made of clay.

It's not alone. There's a fucking regiment of them. Terracotta warriors flanking a hallway eddying in a haze of red light, their features molded into expressions of stern nobility, clay fangs bared. It's as if they're ushering me not into some secret burial chamber, but into the past. Into my old life.

Beyond, at the end of the hallway, a seductive red glare beckons, like that of a Shanghai nightclub.

When I swallow, my throat clicks. The doors groan shut behind me, and the pop and fizzle of the fireworks cuts out, sealing me in darkness and silence. All I can hear is the blood booming in my ears. All I can hear is a voice inside me warning, *Don't go in there. Go back. This is a mistake.*

Balling my hands at my sides, I march down the corridor flanked by statues of the undead and into *The Palace of the Fang*.

It's another world. I've seen many casinos in my time: in London, Macau, Singapore, the Bahamas. But this is something else. It's a fever dream of sumptuously carved archways, decorative wood screens, golden wall panels writhing with dragons. Colonnades and wood beams soar above and murals splash across the walls, depicting red-eyed, bat-shaped things swooping above cliff walls hung with coffins.

No bright, flashing slot machines here. That's not what *The Palace of the Fang* offers.

That's when I see the gambling tables, and an old heat pulses behind my eyes, making them itch. The red velvet looks like flayed flesh. Shadows in crisp suits crowd around them, teeth and eyes shining in the light from alluring red silk lanterns. Playing cards fan on the rich cloth, and women in embroidered dresses with captive eyes pass from owner to owner. A head dips to scent a neck, cheeks dimpling in pleasure, and a woman swallows and darts me a look of panicked terror from under her winged lashes.

My heart clenches in my chest, a hard anger throbbing in me like a stroke. Of course. Yes. This is why they come here. This is what they wager. These are the stakes here.

But not for me. Mine are of an altogether different kind.

It takes a great effort to come back to myself. I can't linger here, I know. I'm already attracting attention.

High cruel nostrils sniff, scenting my living blood, and heads turn toward me. I can feel the suspicion, the danger, drawing tight as a bowline knot around me. I have to find Pongshu and get out of here. Now. But where is he? How am I to ever find him amongst all these—

"Pongshu!" a bored voice exclaims. "Must we be so crude?"

There. Beyond the gambling hall is a VIP room, glimpsed through an archway carved into a springing dragon. The room is dim, circular, alcoved with stone sarcophagi standing like sentinels around a solitary table.

A man stands on the table.

At least, I think he's a man. He looks like a damn kid with a K-pop star's androgynous beauty, his fashion gender-fluid: A shock of jet-black hair that sweeps in a curtain against a delicately featured face. A women's pink Chanel jacket over a men's white T-shirt. Glam earrings and pearl necklaces. His rapper-style sneakers knock over piles of casino chips as he sways on the table with a melodramatic flourish of his arms. He is completely sloshed. "I have nothing left to wager, no?" he slurs in a voice as slippery as his frame. He starts pulling off flashy knuckle rings and dropping them onto the table in a series of childish pauses. "Then I"—*plunk*—"go up here"—*plunk*—"with other stakes." A final *plunk* as he giggles down at his competitors at the table, two shark-faced men in suits that couldn't be more opposite from his.

But they aren't looking at him. Because they have caught sight of me.

Pongshu twists about to follow their gaze and flops a wrist. "Fuck are you?"

For a moment, the cards, the casino chips, the red velvet of the table—all of it shimmers like a mirage, like an oasis in the desert, luscious and unreal, and I feel that old addiction stir in me. I shove it down with vicious force and lift my chin.

"The guy sent to take you home," I growl in reply and march forward, come-hithering my fingers. "Come on. Let's go."

A crooked smirk seams Pongshu's face as he studies me carefully avoiding looking at the gambling table. "Oooh," he breathes in a smooth, seductive whisper. "We have an addict here." He hunkers down on the table until he's on his haunches, forearms on knees, and tilts his pretty head over on its side. "It been long time?"

This little fucker's more perceptive than he looks.

But then, one addict can always spot another, can't they?

I grimace and glance away, and Pongshu lets out a peal of delighted laughter and sits himself cross-legged on the table amongst the casino chips, rubbing his hands together. "Tell you what. I'll come with you if you win me in game."

My God, the Steward must have the patience of a saint. I grab for the kid's arm. "Let's go."

"Excuse me, sir." The words are soft, cultured, but I'm smart enough to recognize the deadliness in them. One of the pale-faced poker players dusts the ash off his cigar and weaves a trail of smoke through the air. "This one"—he jabs the glowing end at Pongshu—"owes us a considerable debt, which must be paid. But if you won this round . . ." He shrugs and leans back in his chair. "We would be willing to call it even."

Pongshu moves. He's offering me something: a fan of cards. "You can use my hand."

Our eyes lock. His black ones glitter with devilish amusement. It makes me want to smack them out of his skull.

But I can't help but look at the cards again, imagining the feel of them in my hand once more. The plastic snap of them. The raised texture of the designs on their backs as familiar as the body of a lover.

How naïve I was, to think I'd ever truly kicked it. That eternal addiction. I feel it uncoil in my gut like a slumbering python, ready to unhinge its jaws and swallow me whole again. I can feel the eyes of the gamblers on me. I can feel Pongshu's. And I see myself do it. I see myself lift a trembling hand and reach for the cards . . .

The tips of Pongshu's fangs show in a smile.

"No."

And I retract my hand into a fist.

The players at the table cock eyebrows. Pongshu's smirk slides right off his face.

I square my shoulders. "Do you know who this is?" I say, gesturing.

The players do not take their eyes from me.

"Do you not see the signet ring on his left hand?"

For Pongshu does have a ring there, the only one he left on his hands. Old and gold, with a fancy S graven on its face. Pongshu rolls his eyes and tries to hide it.

"This is the blood son of the Steward," I announce.

If I wasn't looking closely, I would miss the flicker of fear behind those eyes. But I am looking.

It's all I can do not to smile.

"The Steward has charged me with bringing him back." I lean forward, eyes narrowed. "I'm not on close terms with the Steward, but I'd imagine he wouldn't take kindly to anyone intervening with his wishes."

After a long moment, the poker players eye each other, eye me, a low hiss escaping their sharp mouths.

"Glad we have an understanding." I grab Pongshu's elbow and haul him off the table, sending a deluge of casino chips tumbling and bouncing off the hardwood floor.

"So rough," Pongshu admires as he staggers drunkenly in my grip, and I can't tell if he's mocking me or coming onto me. I only pray we're not attracting too much attention as we march toward the casino entrance. As if reading my thoughts, Pongshu scoops a fruity cocktail off the tray of a passing waiter and I pluck it out of his hand and return it. Pongshu pouts and promptly grabs another. "We can both have one. Here." He pushes the drink in my face and I'm hit with that sweet sugarcane smell, that nostril-stinging burn of alcohol, deadly and redolent of temptation. It's like shoving a stick of burning dynamite in my face.

I don't think. I smack it away, sending the contents sloshing into the air.

Heads turn our way. Pongshu hunches his own down into his shoulders, makes a face like "Daddy's angry" and hands the cocktail off. "An alcoholic, too."

I don't care. I push onward through the crowd, unheeding of the looks we're getting. A black temper is beginning to gather around me like a fog: I'm already over this babysitting job. But we're nearly there. We're past the gambling tables now and entering that corridor lined with the terracotta undead. Pongshu slows to trail a hand across their armor and coos "Hellooo" before I tug him on. Ahead are those round double doors with their inlay of teeth. Only a minute now. One more minute and we'll be out of here and boarding that blasted sampan. One more minute and I'll be on my way back to Mrs. Colding—

"Captain Redfearn?"

My insides clench.

And when I turn, a shadow stands at the end of the corridor behind us, legs planted apart and hands in pockets, dressed in a tux that does nothing to hide the violent nature contained within. "Well, well, it is you," the shadow rumbles, and steps forward. "Come to gamble with the dead, have we?"

SEVENTEEN
MRS. COLDING

It takes a moment for it to set in. The import of it.

Once I was on deck and at the bow, I noticed a yacht had nosed up to the tunnel leading to *The Palace of the Fang*, as if standing guard. And it's only now that the lit-up nameplate registers, making my stomach drop.

It says *House of Shadows*.

"Oh no," I breathe.

EIGHTEEN
CAPTAIN REDFEARN

"Nothing to say, capitaine?" the mercenary hired by Lair Yachting, Inc. asks as he strides down the corridor.

We're alone. The casino behind hums on in its delirium of whispers and red light, a world away. No one has noticed. Only Pongshu furrows his brow at me, failing to comprehend due to the fuck-ton of alcohol altering his brain.

I draw myself up. "I think you've mistaken me for someone else."

I don't wait for a response from this killer. I turn on my heel and push through one of the double doors, hearing the mercenary sprinting after me. I've barely made it down the front steps of the casino before the voice booms behind me. "Captain Redfearn!"

There's no ignoring that. I halt on the landing stage and shut my eyes, cursing under my breath. The casino guards, the sampan pilots, the commuting guests—all stare at us.

When I turn about, the mercenary is descending the casino steps.

"So rude," he tuts in his suave Franco-Algerian accent, and it's now that I remember his name from Hibernacula: Mr. Lelouch. "Leaving a party without taking a dance."

I shake my head. "I don't think you'd enjoy dancing with me."

The mercenary drops off the last step and sizes me up, a dark pleasure in his eyes. "Don't get me excited." He looks left and right, taking in the bystanders, the casino with its lights and gabled roofs, the cliff walls hung with coffins in their hundreds, and a small smile flits about his lips. "I don't see how you're getting out of this, capitaine."

I meet his eyes. "The young don't see a lot of things."

Fireworks explode in those dark irises. Cheeks lift in a smile.

Pongshu looks between us, struck sober at last.

This Lelouch is even quicker than I thought he'd be: one hand sweeps away his tux jacket to reveal a Glock in a shoulder holster, right where I knew it would be, and his other blurs toward that black polymer grip.

But *they* are faster than either of us.

The sound is deafening. It hits us in a rumble of sound, a symphony of pops and creaks as hundreds of wooden lids are pushed up. And when the mercenary and I crane our heads skyward, we see every last one of the undead above us are halfway out of their coffins, the glare of the fireworks catching in their glowing eyes and on the bone of their claws gripping lid and frame.

Lelouch slowly, slowly removes his hand from his gun, and I grin. "No blood spilled on palace grounds," I remind him.

A muscle twitches under the mercenary's eye and he bellies up to me, noses almost touching. "See you soon, capitaine."

I smirk, my eyes not leaving his as I back away, Pongshu's arm gripped tightly in my hand. Hundreds of eyes follow our every move. The only sound the pop and fizz of the fireworks above. "Get in," I growl, and Pongshu dutifully clambers into the empty boat I've backed us up to, dumping himself in the floor with a giggle when I let him go. The mercenary takes his time. He only walks up to his own boat as I hop in and start the motor. And as *The Palace of the Fang* recedes like a fiery fever dream as we enter that tunnel again, that other boat begins to follow.

I sit there in the sampan as it scrapes along in the dark and try to slow my breathing, taking stock of things.

At the bow, Pongshu sprawls between the red silk lanterns swinging from their poles, their light crazed and leaping on his genderless face. He's grinning.

"What you going to do . . . *Captain Redfearn?*"

Beyond him, at the far end of the tunnel, a yacht is waiting. And it's not the *Thing*.

Behind us, Lelouch's boat is approaching the other end.

And here we are, midway down the tunnel that's just wide enough to let one boat squeeze through at a time, its rock walls claustrophobically close on either side.

There's only one play here.

I cut the engine and look at Pongshu. "Blow out the lanterns."

The kid cocks his head, his long, curved canines showing as an almost admiring smirk twists his mouth. And he obeys.

That mercenary is going fast—much too fast—which I've counted on. He's on top of us before he knows what's happening. The little lanterns swinging at his bow only show our stopped boat blocking the tunnel at the last moment. A split second before his sampan crashes into ours in an awful splintering of wood, I leap, and I must look like some nightmare springing out of the depths of his subconscious.

"Shit," he hisses.

But I've already landed on him, grabbing at the Glock he's somehow already drawn. And then the tunnel is filled with the sound of thunder.

NINETEEN
MRS. COLDING

For a moment, I don't understand the flash that lights up the jagged silhouette of that tunnel. Then there's the sharp pop that makes me jump, and a black cloud of bats streams out into the night.

A gunshot. That was a gunshot.

My heart rabbits in my chest. I have to swallow down a blinding sheen of tears. I can't think that way. I can't.

There's the footstep of a deckhand behind me, and I whirl. "Lift anchor and get us closer. We need to be ready to leave the moment he returns. Move!" Then I turn back to that tunnel, heart aching, wanting to pull out of my skin.

"Redfearn," I breathe. "Please be okay."

TWENTY

CAPTAIN REDFEARN

The crack of that gunshot deafens me.

My ears fill with a high tinnitus sound. The tunnel lights up with a blinding flash and then everything is a tornado of fluttery black shapes, mouselike squeaks, light leaping wildly from the swinging lanterns of the mercenary's boat. For a moment my heart clenches and I think of Penelope, of Mrs. Colding, and wait for the pain to come.

But it didn't hit me.

The bullet ricochets off the tunnel walls in a blast of sparks, a zigzag of light through that whirling passage of bats, and I remember that I'm fighting for my life.

Lelouch is younger, faster, stronger, and so I know experience will be my only advantage here. We grapple over the gun and fists and knees fly as we redirect its aim between us. It goes off again and again, those barks of fire freeze-framing our silhouettes in choreographies of violence in that narrow space. A haymaker catches me in the ribs, driving the wind out of me, and Lelouch grabs my head and bangs it hard against the tunnel wall.

That sharp flare of pain changes everything.

The old rage snaps into place, bringing on a ferocious clarity. I dodge his following combo of strikes, kick downward and blow out his knee in a crunch of cartilage. He grunts and I grab the gun with both hands over his, hop into the air with both feet planted on his torso, and push. Within the space of a second, I've pinned him against the tunnel rock with my back braced against the opposite wall, the bore of the gun trained at his head.

Lelouch's face slackens. "Wait—"

The shot blows his brains out across the rock in a leap of gore.

I stay there braced in the air against the corpse, trying to catch my breath and dismiss the onset of a queasy disquiet.

"Dear me," says a voice, startling me, and I drop into the boat and whirl with gun held tight in front of me.

Pongshu squats on the outboard motor of our boat like some goatish horror, brushing specks of skull off his Chanel jacket. "That came easy, didn't it?"

Cold blossoms in my gut.

"You are like me," he goes on in a vicious, loving whisper, and there's a casino chip dancing across his knuckles now, glinting gold in the lanternlight. "All rage and addiction. Because deep down you know you not worthy of love."

And the poker chip halts its progress across his knuckles as he smiles at me.

That cold spreads down into my bones, making itself at home, and I don't need to turn to see that my antic shadow on the rock wall of the tunnel is that of a Navy SEAL in a tactical wetsuit.

But I don't have time to dwell on that.

A rectangle of light glows on in the jacket of the mercenary's corpse slumped in the floor of the sampan. His phone. It's ringing.

I answer it.

"Sir?" A man's crackling voice. "Is he there?"

I take a moment to clear my throat, the stench of gunsmoke and brain matter still in my nostrils. Then I try my best imitation of Lelouch's growly-smooth Franco-Algerian accent. "Negative. Just having a round at the poker tables. Back soon." I hang up and toss the phone into the water. That should buy us some time.

I'm about to shove the Glock into the back of my pants when I look down.

Pongshu has flowed over into the boat with me and is crouching over Lelouch's body, his teeth fastened in its throat.

A roil of disgust fills me. I shut my eyes, take in a long, steadying breath. "Let's go," I order and pull at him, and there's a snarl and Pongshu whips his head at me, fangs bared and eyes completely black, blood dripping from his chin.

An icy stillness settles over me.

I place the barrel of the Glock against Pongshu's ivory forehead and lean forward. "Don't. Push me," I breathe.

After what seems like forever, that bloodlust clears in Pongshu's eyes and he rises, dragging a pink sleeve of his jacket across his chin, leaving a red smear there. "Yes," he says, nodding. "You like me."

He flows like a cat back onto our boat, and I wait until he's at the bow before I stash the Glock and follow.

The motor takes a couple of tries before she catches, and I rev her up and floor her, leaving all sight of that casino behind. A sudden certainty hits me that that's not the last time I'll see *The Palace of the Fang*. That it's not done with me yet. That one day I'll be drawn back into its hallucinatory maze of sin and temptation. Then we're rushing out of darkness, out of the tunnel into night and fresh air. And past that dead mercenary's unwitting yacht is the *Thing* waiting for us with its generators humming and Mrs. Colding standing on the swim deck with tears of relief in her eyes. That sweet woman who does not yet know who I truly am. What I am capable of. What darknesses I have yet inside me.

Pongshu in the bow looks back at me, a smarmy smirk on his lips, and I know he's thinking the same thing. And that he can't wait for her to find out.

TWENTY-ONE
MRS. COLDING

If I'd had any doubts about how much I care for Captain Redfearn, they are completely dispelled now.

I pace on the *Thing*'s swim deck as I wait for him to emerge from the tunnel leading to *The Palace of the Fang*. I can barely keep my composure intact. My heart is in my throat. I can barely breathe. I am out of my wits with worry. I hold my hands to my chest, my throat, feeling my heart wanting to pound out of it. When I see the sampan gun out of the tunnel with Redfearn at the tiller, I feel my head go light with pins and needles. The relief is so blindingly intense it's all I can do not to vomit.

And as he sweeps up to the swim deck, all I want to do is rush to him and make sure he's okay. He wasn't harmed. He wasn't shot.

But I can't. We don't have time for that.

As soon as they hop onto the deck, I unclip the crew radio at my hip. "They're aboard. Get us out of here."

The *Thing*'s stern thrusters kick in, swirling the sampan away in a roil of foam as the *Thing* hightails it away from the cliff. Redfearn doesn't even bother glancing behind—he's all business.

The first thing he does is push his guest toward the deckhands who are with me. "Escort him to one of the guest suites," he orders. Then he's leaning to whisper in my ear, and it takes everything in me to concentrate on his words. "Make sure he stays out of the way."

I glance at the guest. Pongshu is not what I expected—a little model of a bloodsucker in clothes of mixed gender, slippery and scornful and pretty as a pop star, reeking of blood and rice wine. As he's marched past me, he gives me a leering, knowing smirk that makes my flesh crawl.

This one's gonna be trouble.

"Aiiiyaaaaa," he marvels. "Didn't you a bag lovely piece of ass."

Redfearn jabs a finger. "Get him the fuck out of here."

I ignore this, heat rushing to my forehead. "What about you?" I ask, barely feeling my tingling lips. Redfearn's tux is rumpled, but I don't see any bullet holes in it. And I can't tell if the blood freckling his face and pleated white tuxedo shirt belong to him or not.

Redfearn looks off to the *House of Shadows* still waiting by the tunnel. "I need to make sure we get out of here safely."

I scan the deck, making sure we're alone before I lift a hand to the blood trickling from his scalp. He turns to me now. He takes my hand and squeezes it, giving me a pained smile. "I'm okay."

It's enough, for now. Enough for that sick knot in my gut to loosen a little.

"I'll see you in my quarters later," he promises.

"All right," I manage back around the lump in my throat.

I can feel the *Thing* thrumming across the bay and out to open sea as we walk Pongshu into his suite. He collapses onto the bed with a groan, hips cocked up in a ridiculous position, his cheek mashed into the sheets. I've assumed he's passed out by the time I start shutting the door behind me.

"You think you know."

I freeze, one hand on the doorknob, and look back over my shoulder.

A hooded eye is studying me, like a crocodile filming back its eyeball as it studies its prey. His mouth crooks up in a jagged grin, half-lost in the sheets. "You think you know what he is. But you don't."

An ugly flush of anger, dark and immediate, rises up in me. I open my mouth.

But that eye has shut. He's already passed out, snoring into the bed.

I shut the door, angry with myself. Angry that I'd allow a creature like that to put doubt into my mind about Captain Redfearn.

I knock gently on the door to his quarters near the wheelhouse. I haven't seen them before.

"Come in," he grunts.

The space is small, cramped, not like the full-beam guest suites. There's a writing desk with nothing but his logbook on it, its back made up of a few cubbyholes stuffed with navigation charts. It's all very, very tidy. I don't know if that's a product of his yachting and Navy years, or if he always keeps his quarters that way for my benefit, knowing I'd be itching to clean if I stepped foot inside.

The only other thing in there is the bed, big enough to almost take up the entire quarters.

And a shirtless Captain Redfearn is wincing as he lowers himself onto it.

I wasn't prepared for this. The shock of it makes my cheeks burn. Then I see the bruises already starting to blossom on his ribs and face, and I hiss in air.

"I'll get some ice," I say, turning.

"No. Just—" He shakes out a handful of painkillers, knocks them back. "Help me."

I take the bottle of Ibuprofen and set it on the nightstand, ease him back down into the bed. He grunts once, hard, then lets out a long breath and looks up at me. "Thank you. There's no sign of the *House of Shadows* following us. I think we're in the clear."

I give him a moment before I ask it. "What happened back there?"

He shrugs, then grimaces at the movement. "That mercenary spotted us in the casino. Barely got out alive, but . . . I knew if he got out too, he wouldn't stop being a threat."

I already know the answer, but Pongshu's words are reverberating in my head. I have to ask it.

"So what did you do?"

Captain Redfearn looks up at me, and he can't hide the naked apprehension there. "What I had to."

I nod, once, swallowing hard and pushing down an old feeling of panic. He sees it and reaches for my hand. "I'm not proud of it. But there was nothing else for it."

"I know. I understand." I look down at his big hand rubbing mine, and his knuckles are scraped raw, swollen black with bruises. The hand of a killer.

My own hand begins to shake. I open my mouth, ready to tell him that I'm struggling. That those old fears of not feeling safe I had around Mr. Colding are bubbling back up to the surface. But when I look up, he's already shut his eyes, has succumbed to exhaustion and fallen into a deep sleep.

TWENTY-TWO
CAPTAIN REDFEARN

I wake with a start to the sound of women shrieking.

I jolt upright, my whole body flaring with pain. I have to hold my throbbing skull a moment before I can concentrate again.

It's the girls. The Asian girls picked up in Hong Kong. They're shrieking.

A chill prickles all the way down to the base of my spine.

I lurch out of my quarters, still buttoning my white yachtie polo as I slide back the glass door of the bridge deck and take in the sight.

We've stopped at sea. It's midday, the sun blazing down, and a giant inflatable slide has been hooked onto the yacht. One by one, bikini-clad girls are rushing down it into the water, splashing and shrieking with laughter.

And Pongshu is there, in the shade of the bridge deck awning, watching them like a predator lurking at a watering hole.

And not just watching. The girls are coming up to him, fawning over his women's clothing, his jewelry, his anime-perfect hair. And it hits me now that his femme looks are calculated for this very reason. He doesn't give a damn about the style. He finds it disgusting. He's only using it to lure women to him, using their own fashion against them to bring them into the palm of his hand, all the while mocking them.

"Chanel," he announces to his audience, pinching his jacket. "I could get a you. Have to be my girl, though."

The girls giggle, and my insides constrict in repugnance and rage.

Bing saunters up the stairs to the aft bridge deck, sleek-haired and dripping water after her slide, and my blood stops. She catches sight of Pongshu and blushes.

No.

She's barely started toward him before I step between.

"Hey," she says, brow furrowed, and squints at my face. "Youuuu okay?"

I dab at my temple, am reminded of last night by the sting of bruises there. "Oh. Yeah. Just . . . got into the wrong crowd last night."

"Uh-huh." She cranes to look around me at Pongshu, and I clear my throat.

"Have you thought about leaving the modeling industry?" I blurt out.

She narrows her eyes at me. "Why?"

It takes everything I have to not glance at Pongshu. "There are some bad people in that industry."

She chews her lip, trying to figure me out. "And go back home? Have father tell me what to do?" She snorts and crosses her arms. "Fuck him. As if he miss me."

I think of a six-year-old Penelope watching me walk out the door for my next charter and feel a sharp pang in my chest.

"Hey." The word makes Bing meet my eyes. "Maybe he misses you more than you think."

Bing screws her face up, studying me, and backs away. "Whatever." She turns, says something in Mandarin to a friend, and they jump down the slide together, shrieking and giggling.

"Don't worry."

I stiffen. Pongshu, cocktail in hand, stands at my elbow.

"I won't touch merchandise," he promises. He swirls his cocktail, grins as he brings it to his lips. "At least, not before I see Father."

I snort, not feeling reassured in the slightest.

Pongshu leans a convivial elbow on my shoulder. "That one," he says, pointing at a slim girl in a monokini as she passes by. "Think I let her suck me off before I rip throat open, fuck it with my cock." He tilts his head over to study me closely. "What you think of that?"

I stare straight ahead, willing a muscle twitching at my eye to be still. "What I think doesn't matter."

A delicious smirk curls up one side of Pongshu's face. "You no like a me much, do you, captain?"

I resist the urge to shrug that fucking elbow off me, my hands balling at my sides.

Pongshu sees it; nothing escapes him. His eyes glitter with the knowledge. "No," he snorts, with something very much like gloating triumph. "Everyone no like a mirror."

He rests his chin on top of his elbow, inches from me. "You know why I see you, captain? We poker players. Have to see into heart of opponent." He thumps my chest, making me flinch. "A poker game as intimate as lovemaking. And like love, at end there always a little death." He finally slides off me and I shrug that shoulder in disgust, teeth gritted.

But he's not done. He's produced something from that damnable pink Chanel jacket: a deck of cards. "Care for game?"

I feel my muscles tighten, my blood grow hot in my veins. I turn away.

"Aiiiyaaaaa," Pongshu whines with innocent malice. "No take a joke?" He shoves his cocktail at a stewardess without looking at her, accordions the deck of cards between his hands in a blur. "You like me, remember?"

That stops me in my tracks.

"You gamble to put order on what has no order. But there nothing out there. Rocks spinning mindlessly in a cold dark. The awful chaos of existence." The cards spring and collapse in on themselves. Hypnotic. Menacing. "Your rage? Despair? Self-hatred?" He waggles a finger. "No controlling that. That never change. Never go away." He is at my ear now, pouring his poison into it in a seething whisper. "You always be like a this. Like me. Only fooling yourself if you believe otherwise." And now, flashing at me again: his wicked smile. "So. Care for game?"

His taunting laughter follows me as I stalk away.

"How are you feeling?" Mrs. Colding asks, and then she sees me and her face falls. "Oh."

I've found her below deck in the guest suites, directing the stews at doing heads and beds while the guests are at their watersports. I jerk my head and she follows me into the privacy of the lower deck saloon, the glass-bottomed infinity pool shimmering above us.

"I don't trust that shit stain for a second," I growl in opening. "He's practically drooling over the models. We need to get them off the boat before something happens."

"How, though?" Mrs. Colding asks. "How do we do that without Pongshu knowing? And what excuse will we use when we see the Steward?"

I shake my head. I don't know.

There's a shriek and splash, and I glance out a porthole to the bouncy swoop of color that's the water slide. "We'll stay here for the day, let them have their fun. It'll give us time to come up with a plan."

Mrs. Colding waits, watching me. She always knows.

"What is it?" she finally asks.

I run a hand down my face, pinch my eyes. "Being forced to resort to this . . . violence again . . ." My pulse bangs in my temples. I have to swallow before I go on. "It's bringing back a lot of . . . and Pongshu . . ." Shame fills my throat, sealing it shut. I can't go on. It's too much, in this moment, to show her what I've hidden from myself for years.

Mrs. Colding studies me a long time, turning something over in her mind as refractions of light from the pool play over her face. Then she pronounces, quite calmly, "Whatever it is, you need to work through it, Redfearn."

I nod. I know.

"I can help you through it, but I can't fix you. You're responsible for that yourself."

I can feel my cheeks burning.

She sighs, clasps her hands before her. "The first step is recognizing where it comes from," she goes on, her tone very gentle. "I've seen you writing in that logbook of yours. Maybe it'd be helpful to write this down. Get it out."

I nod and smile to myself, as embarrassed as a dressed-down stew. Yet through it all, tender with gratitude and somehow surprised, after all this time, that she has the solution to everything.

"See you in my quarters later?" I offer. "At sundown?"

She gifts me with her smile. "At sundown."

CAPTAIN'S LOG

Off Mainland Coast of China, December 11th.
Ship: *Thing.*
Speed: At anchor.
Weather: Clear day.
Notes: I don't know where to start.
Mrs. Colding always knows the right thing to do, though.
So I'll put my faith in her.

It began with my father, I suppose. A curt man. An angry man. A black cloud whose mood could sour the whole house. Nothing was ever enough for him. Back then, I was fat. No getting around it. Food was a way to escape my life, though I couldn't have put words to it back then. Perhaps it was also to spite my father. He had been an athlete. Prided himself on his physical prowess, his college football medals he still dusted once a week and kept sparkling on his shelf.

And me? I was an oaf. A curly-haired nerd picked last for school sports. A disappointment.

And so when I asked for a little money so I could move to another city for state college, he asked what for. To study writing, I told him. I wanted to be an author. Write some of those fantasy books I spent my life reading and which had given me an escape, just like my eating had. My father put on a puss and said, *What do you have to write about? May as well use that paper to wipe my ass, if you want to be useful.* Then he said if I wanted to get a *real* education, I should do what he did and join the marines. Lose that baby fat and get a real haircut.

I boarded a bus first thing in the morning so my mother wouldn't see me crying.

And I did enlist, though I did my father one better. I became a Navy SEAL, something my father never managed. He flunked out of BUD/S and had nursed that wound ever since. I didn't wash out. My father had been too entitled, had thought too highly of himself, to hack it. For all his bluster, he had been given everything his whole life. It wasn't like that with the Navy SEALs. There, every man—no matter his station in life before he got there—was treated the same. And his worth could only be proved by how much he could endure and overcome.

My father never stood a chance.

Not me. I had enough anger in me to get me through anything they threw at me. Shivering for hours as I lay in the drowning surf linked arm-and-arm with my teammates. Brutal physical conditioning that pushed me past the point of endurance, and which left me shaking and puking on the edge of the gym mat. I shaved my head, shredded my body down to a hard core of grit and muscle. During deployment I took up surfing to stay in shape. And the operations allowed me to unleash my rage in a cool, detached way that I could justify as defensible because of its military sanctioning.

This is what I wanted. I wanted to become a man who was lean and cool and bad to the bone. I wanted to come home a man remade, someone my parents didn't recognize. A man who had attained what my father couldn't. And when I'd finally get his approval, I would reject it, drive off without a word to show him how much I didn't need him. Didn't need his love.

After my tour, I flew home brimming with arrogant pride, my Special Operations rating badge pinned to the blouse of my Navy fatigues.

But the house was empty. A "For Sale" sign in the yard.

They died in a car crash, a neighbor told me. A year earlier. It was instantaneous.

They didn't suffer.

I didn't know what to do. This had been my plan. This had been how I'd counted on getting closure, of ridding myself of the poisonous anger that had infected me ever since I could remember.

Now, all that was compounded with even more guilt and shame, and with nowhere to put it.

So I left again, this time to become a yacht captain. To become a sailor, like all my favorite authors had been, free at last to be whoever I wanted to be.

But that rage and despair never fully went away. I thought it would with marriage, having a child. How would that not fulfill a man? For a time, it did. For a time, I was able to forget. But it wasn't enough. I had never worked through that curse my father gave me. Never got to the root of it. That festering sense of shame and failure that clung to me like a namesake. An unwanted inheritance. A flaw in my genes. And slowly but surely I took on more and more yacht charters, stayed away from home for longer and longer stretches at a time.

I didn't want to, Pen. I wanted to be there for you.

I remember. God, I remember. The self-hate I was taught that drove me away, thinking I didn't deserve love. You clinging to me every time I left for a charter. Your mother's accusing stare in the hallway. It was too much to bear. I began to slip out—God help me—without saying goodbye to you. Sneaking out of my own home like a thief. How you must have hated me. Your mother sure as hell did. *You're hurting her*, she seethed. *Why can't you just disappear entirely and spare her the pain?*

So I did.

I thought I was doing you a kindness. I thought you'd be better off without me. *I* thought I'd be better off without me.

And now you have disappeared, too. Maybe out of love for me, maybe out of hate. Maybe both.

I knew one day there would be the strange, humiliating desolation of your child abandoning you. Moving on, embarking on their own lives, coming to a place where they have no use for you. Such is life.

But I didn't expect this. I didn't expect it to happen this way. That you would turn against me. Renounce me.

That's what it feels like, anyway. Maybe this is your way of showing me that you have.

And now I know. This is what it's like to feel abandoned. To have your family—your own child, your own blood—disappear at sea.

A vanishing act, meant to wound. To hurt. A lesson.

Just like I had done with my father. My family. The circle complete.

This is what I have passed down. I thought I would break the cycle. I thought I would be different.

But I'm not.

There's hope yet, though. I can correct this course. I can make this right.

I promised you, after all.

I'll find you, Pen. I'll find both of us. We're here. We exist.

We deserve love.

TWENTY-THREE
MRS. COLDING

At sundown, I knock on the door to Captain Redfearn's quarters.

I've spent the day wracking my brain on how to solve our dilemma. How to get the models to safety and corral this troublemaking fiend we've picked up. But it's been difficult to keep my thoughts from straying. Because at the back of my mind, all I can think of is Captain Redfearn. What has he written down in that logbook? Will he be able to open up to me in person? I know he has his struggles. That he has a history of violence and addiction. And I know that if he can't face this thing, we'll never be able to be together.

The thought gives me an unbearable pang of loss.

Please, I think. *Please find a way, Captain Redfearn. Please be the man I need you to be.*

"Come in," he says.

He's still sitting at his writing desk when I enter. He closes the logbook and turns to me, and I try to read the expression on his face. He looks . . . humbled. Worn out. Chastened. But also relieved. As if part of a burden has been taken off his shoulders, some old wound purified.

He looks wiser.

When he sees me, though, his face changes. I may have put on a tad more makeup, a subtle tint of lipstick, in preparation for this meeting. As if we were going out on a date.

Captain Redfearn lurches out of his chair, sucks up his jaw with a click. "Care for a drink?" he stammers at last.

"I'm fine." I smile, blushing. "Thank you."

But he won't take no for an answer. He waves a dismissive hand. "You've been stressed all day. Here." He opens the small fridge by his bed and pulls out a red soda can, hands it to me. "I know you like one when you need a boost."

I look down at the can. It's a Coca-Cola, its swirling white font looking like a promise of happiness.

I take it with a blush, glimpse a row of these cans stacked inside the fridge door before he shuts it again.

He keeps that fridge stocked with them. Just for me. Just on the off-chance I need one.

How well he knows me.

My blush deepens, and he gestures again for us to sit on the edge of the bed. To cover my awkwardness, I pull the tab on the can, take a sip of that crisp, refreshing fizz of sugar. Does he know? That as a girl this was my introduction to America? That on special occasions my father would give me a Coke, and it was like I was being offered a taste of the American dream?

Back then, it tasted like freedom. And now, as an adult, it tastes like childhood.

I can never get enough of it.

I hold the Coke in my lap and glance at Captain Redfearn. He doesn't know where to put his eyes. He looks away from my lips, my made-up face, then away from my bare legs in my yachtie skirt, and harrumphs deep in his throat.

"I've been thinking," he begins, a little unsteady. "And I know what to do." I wait as he gathers himself. "We turn Pongshu's love of drink against him. We get him blackout drunk and get the models off the boat while he's unconscious."

I purse my lips, take another sip of my Coke. "Doesn't sound overly difficult. But when we get to the Steward without his cargo?"

Captain Redfearn allows himself a rakish grin. "Our solution may have fallen into our lap: We trade the Steward's blood son for my daughter."

I lift my brows. "That's . . . risky." And I allow a small smirk to twist my mouth. "But it just might work."

He beams.

I can't help it: My gaze strays to the logbook on the desk, and he catches me. His expression turns serious. "I've also . . . been thinking of other things."

I wait, clutching the cold can hard between my knees, my heart fluttering against my ribs.

He turns on the bed to face me. "This voyage," he says. "This mission to get Penelope back . . . It's forced me to do things I haven't done in a long time. Things I'm not proud of, and which are coming back to me far too easily. And that has brought back with it old fears, old weaknesses, old anger . . ." A vein throbs on his brow. He has to drop his head and swallow before he goes on.

You can do it, Redfearn.

"I'm scared, Mrs. Colding. I'm scared of what I will become. Of what kind of man I'll have to turn into to get my daughter back. I'm scared I'll lose myself to . . . to this shame my father gave me. The idea that I . . . that I don't deserve . . ." He lets out a bitter laugh and shakes his head, rubs at his black and blue knuckles. "It's ridiculous, but I'm scared that Pongshu fucker's right. That I'm just like him."

How different, I think. *How different he is from Mr. Colding.*

He worries so much about how he treats others. How good a person he is. I can trust that.

I can trust a man like that.

I can trust him.

I can be *with him.*

"Oh, Captain Redfearn," I pronounce at last. "You are nothing like that manipulative little creature."

His head jerks up, and I see a glassy sheen in his eyes, a leaping of joy and relief at my absolution.

I set the Coke on the nightstand and take his hand in both of mine, dropping his eyes there. "You're a good person," I tell him, squeezing hard. "And you deserve love. You *are* loved."

He stills all over. His eyes find mine again. Waiting.

So I say it, the words loosed like beautiful birds from my mouth.

"I love you, Captain Redfearn."

My heart is pounding away in my breast, my head so light I feel like I might pass out. But he is smiling. I have never seen him smile like this. It is as if he is a boy again, brought back to a time when the world hummed with goodness. And that sheen in his eyes is building up, gathering at the bottoms of his eyes as he says, "I love you too, Mrs. Colding. I've loved you since the moment I saw you two years ago."

It's too much. I hiccup something that's halfway between a laugh and a sob and hold a hand to my mouth. I'm blinded by a sudden welling of tears.

He smiles, soft, tender, and swipes the tears from under my eyes with his thumbs. And they keep moving, swooping back across my cheeks in a rhythmic, comforting way. His eyes—storm-gray, pearled with light—curve in amusement.

When his hands dip lower, onto my throat, to where Evangeline bit me—I can't help it.

I flinch.

Captain Redfearn sees it. He stills, catching my eyes again, as if asking for permission for something. Then he dips his head, so slowly it feels like an eternity, and touches his lips to those silvery fang-mark scars.

My breath catches. An electric current sizzles through me. My eyes sting again.

He's kissing me there. There at that site of so much pain and trauma. As if he could somehow extract all that from me with his lips. As if he could extract my past—Evangeline's attack, Mr. Colding and all he left me with—and leave everything behind shimmering and cleansed.

As if to say, without words, *You're safe with me*.

His mouth melts against my throat, so tender I have to shut my eyes and bite the inside of my cheek to keep from sobbing. I have never been touched so tenderly.

When I open my eyes again, he's staring at me, my trembling bottom lip. The corner of his mouth curves up, just the slightest bit, and he touches my cupid's bow. My lips part, the pad of his thumb lingering on that bottom lip.

My heart has gone light and jittery in my chest. A heaviness gathers between my thighs. I flick my eyes up into his, caught. I don't know what to think in this moment. All my thoughts have been scattered to the winds.

Then he's dipping his head toward me, never once looking away from my eyes.

Our lips catch lightly, pull away, then slip deeper together. A small noise sighs out of me. I can feel my tears slipping down my cheeks, burning between our faces. I feel as if we've been cast under an enchantment.

I kiss him back, harder now and with a hint of teeth, a burning lunge of need. And he responds, his hands drawing me to him across the bed, my hip against his, my body tucked against his in a sudden engulfing of heat, all my soft parts against his hard parts, his arms caging me, vibrating with power. And I think, *This would be the first time since Mr. Colding.*

I pull back in a sharp gasp of air and shoot to my feet, rubbing two fingers across my lips as if to taste that kiss again, evaluating it and what comes with it.

Behind me, Captain Redfearn watches from the bed, chest heaving and face pale with worry. But waiting.

When I turn to him, fingers still pushing my bottom lip to the side in pouty folds, Redfearn holds his breath.

Then my fingers drop, undoing the buttons of my yachtie shirt, one by one. Steady and all business.

Redfearn's face has colored, his breathing low and harsh as he stares at me, confused but hungry as my shirt begins to part, revealing a deepening glimpse of my cleavage.

When I drop my shirt to the floor, his eyebrows bounce up.

When I unzip my yachtie skirt and shimmy it down my hips and step out of it, his eyebrows have climbed into his hairline.

I stand there, tingling with need and vulnerability before him, and whisper it, a soft but imperious command: "Make love to me, Captain Redfearn."

The captain's gray eyes darken at the words. His throat dips in a swallow, and he rises, strides toward me. Something fluttery catches in my chest. When he stops before me, I look at up at him with my pulse quivering in my throat, not knowing what's going to happen next here.

He lifts his hands, and they go around me. I feel a tugging at my hair, and then bobby pins are bouncing onto the carpet. He's letting my hair down from its bun, letting it flow around my shoulders in a loose swirl of midnight, feeling it in his hands as if it were spun gold, as if something worth worshipping.

One look at his face and my mouth goes dry, my body turning everywhere into hot and cold patches.

He's been wanting to do this for a very long time.

He takes me in, eyes shining, and I suddenly feel shy, held up and honored and set aglow. Then emboldened.

I lift my hands and hold his face between them, rub his cheeks with my thumbs so I can finally feel that stubble rasping under them. I smile.

He smiles back, sweet and hesitant and disbelieving, and I feel as if my chest can't contain this happiness. It wants to crack under the pressure.

Then he cups his hand around my jaw, bunching in my hair, and pulls me to him.

This kiss is different. It's deep, soulful, all-consuming. It takes my breath away. His other hand follows the curve of my back, sweeps me close until all my skin is pressed against him. Heat dumps into me. I curl my fingers into his shirt, tilt my head to the side to accommodate his lips grazing my mouth, my cheek, down my neck, and when he lets out a low, rumbling growl of need it brings a helpless noise out of me in return.

Every part of me is riveted on his hands as they grasp my hips, dive down under the fabric of my panties, gripping up handfuls of flesh. My nipples perk in my bra, tingle and grow hard as they rub against Redfearn pressing against me.

I shiver.

"Please," I whisper, almost begging.

He doesn't make me beg. He scoops me up by my ass, and my legs wrap around his waist, my arms around his neck, as he spins me around and marches me to the bed.

My heart pounds against his. I cannot breathe. I feel almost out of my body with exhilaration.

It's happening. It's really happening. We're finally together. I've finally let him in.

We're finally us.

TWENTY-FOUR
CAPTAIN REDFEARN

"Make love to me, Captain Redfearn."

The words are still ringing in my ears as I lay her down on the bed, her hair laid out for me on the sheets like a dream, like a glorious tumbling of silky darkness. I pick up a strand of it again and feel it between my rough fingers, fingers I've believed for so long didn't deserve to touch such fine a thing. Such a wondrous thing.

But I'm here. And she is lying beneath me, in this bed. She chose me. And she is so, so beautiful in this moment.

With her hair down, she is transformed. That forbidding coldness, that prim and proper façade has been stripped away, revealing what I always knew was beneath: someone giving and purehearted and willful, powerful in their vulnerability. She looks as if she is afire.

My heart clenches painfully in my chest.

She smiles up at me, as if sensing my thoughts, and touches my cheek.

"Do I need to tell you twice, Captain Redfearn?"

Fuck no.

I snake my hand into all that gorgeous hair and dip my tongue between her lips, into aching warmth, and when she moans into my mouth I see shimmering spots of color behind my eyes. Her hands push up under my white yachtie polo, hungry, searching, feeling the smoothness of muscle there, until I'm all goose bumps under her touch. "Why is this still on?" she grumbles in frustration and I laugh, pull the polo over my head and toss it aside. I toe off my deck shoes and socks, unbuckle my khaki shorts and tug them down before crawling back onto the bed. The way she is watching me, almost somber, glowing there among the sheets, makes my blood sizzle in my veins. As I prop myself over her again, she stops me with her touch. Her hands on my bare skin, the etched hardness of my ribcage, the scars I've accumulated over the years, white streaks slashing over my ribs and through the fine golden hairs on my sun-bronzed arms. She is taking me in, drinking me with her eyes, her gaze finally tilting up at my face.

She is seeing me. Truly seeing me.

It's too much. An old, wild fear bolts through me.

I look away.

But she turns my face back with a hand, soft skin sliding through hard stubble. Her voice is very gentle. "You don't need to hide what you are from me, Redfearn."

Something happens in my chest. An ache, so deep I didn't know it was there, cracks and loosens. Heat stings the backs of my eyes. A frantic need ratchets in me, and I lean down to kiss her again, deep and tender, breathing her into me. "Mrs. Colding," I rasp, as if the name has changed in my mouth, taken on new meaning.

"Captain Redfearn," she breathes back.

Her flesh is everywhere, her scent in my nostrils. All I can smell is sandalwood and Asian blossoms.

It is heady, overpowering. I am intoxicated. I am lost.

I am home.

I pin her wrists above her head, begin to nibble her lips as if to devour her. Her fingers entwine with mine, squeezing hard enough to crack bone. She kisses back, hard, almost nipping at me. When I suck on her plump bottom lip, she arches her throat and lets out a long, trembling sigh, her quivering legs wrapping around me. Her fingernails dig into me. I feel her twist and strain and try to pull her hands down as she struggles to control herself.

So I cross her wrists and hold them in place with one hand so I can trail my other down her body.

She responds to it, her body aching up toward my touch. The valley of her breasts breaks out in goose bumps as I graze over it. Her ribcage swells as I trace its laddered shapeliness. Her tummy trembles and writhes as my fingers swirl around her belly button, grasp her hip, raze over her thighs, those sexy-as-hell legs I've been dying to touch for years, leaving a blazing trail down her length.

"Stop torturing me," she whispers.

"But I want to take my time," I growl, my mouth in her cleavage. I pull her bra down, and when my thumb rubs over her nipple, she gasps. "If this is your first time in years, I want it to last."

"I've wanted us for years," she breathes, wrists pulling hard, and I push them back down. "I'm glad we waited. It means so much more now. But I don't know if I can wait any longer."

As if to prove it, her hips roll under me, the friction rubbing my erection against her through our underwear. Blood dumps into my groin, making me throb.

And I can feel it. I can feel how wet she is.

This time, when she pulls her wrists, I let them go. She pulls me down to her mouth, making little noises of hunger and need as she reaches into my black boxer briefs and takes me in her hand.

I break off in a gasp, my brow on hers, and she bites my neck, my collarbone, working her hand up and down. Goddamn, she's driving me crazy.

Still that imperious chief stewardess I've always known: forthright, commanding.

She knows what she wants. Why would it be any different in bed?

I pull my briefs down and she helps me. Then I'm grabbing at the lace of her panties, and she lifts her knees up so I can slide them off her.

We're both shuddering with need, brows touching and half-crazed for each other, by the time I push into her.

She shuts her eyes and sucks in a sharp breath, hanging onto my neck, her knees cradling me. "Fuck," I groan, disbelieving. The closeness, the feeling of being inside her—it's even more exquisite than I thought possible. The happiness, the joy, even more exquisite.

She watches me. She knows exactly what I am thinking. Of course she does.

She places her hands on my chest and gently pushes me back, her smile all wicked promise as she turns her back to me, pressing the sweet curves of her body up against me as we both kneel there in the bed. And sweeping her hair to the side with one hand, she gathers all that gorgeousness into a ponytail and offers it to me, waits for me to fist my hand in it before she sinks down onto all fours and arches the sweet bounty of her ass for me, waiting.

My mouth goes dry. My hand shakes with ravenous desire.

She *knows*. Somehow, she knew this was my fantasy. That I've wanted this hair in my hands for years. That I've wanted *her* like this for years.

"What are you waiting for?" she asks, brows lifted, voice dripping with temptation.

I am so dazed, so drunk on the power of her offering herself to me like this, that it takes me a moment to realize what she's doing.

The wind is almost knocked out of her when I throw her onto her back. She stares up in amazement, opens her mouth.

But I brace myself over her, put a finger to her lips.

"*No*," I order in a gravelly rumble. "You're not allowed to think like that right now. You're not on duty. When you're in my bed, you're no longer a chief stew, and I'm no guest you need to please. Right now, for tonight, I please *you*."

She blinks. She looks as if she still hasn't caught her breath. Then I see the color flame into her cheeks, and everything about her goes soft as a wisp of a smile tugs at one corner of her mouth.

"Then please me," she whispers.

And I do.

I take my time. I feel as if we've slid into a dream as we begin to move together. The world growing soft and dark, shrinking down to the burning cinder of our bodies meeting. My hands roam over her, massaging her curves, making every inch of her feel seen and venerated. She shuts her eyes and pulls me down to her, her breath hot in my ear. "Redfearn," she whispers, over and over. "Redfearn . . ." I take her to the edge, again and again, and then draw back, torturing her with pleasure, until she is trembling and holding her arm over her eyes to hide the tears, biting her forearm to keep the screams in check.

And I know. I know she has never been loved like this. Has never been worshipped like this before.

Mr. Colding had never been capable of that.

I take her nipple between my teeth, swirl my tongue around it until it's long and hard in my mouth and she's gasping at the sensation. I ghost my lips along her jaw, down the sweet curve of her neck to those fang-mark scars again, until she isn't even aware of them anymore. I have blurred them away with my love.

Her fingers slide down me, digging into my buttocks, pulling me deeper. She writhes and tilts her hips under me, grinding against me, lost in her passion. And when she finally comes, over and over, she cries out with abandon, holding nothing back now, shuddering and laughing and letting the tears scorch down her cheeks.

No. Not cold. She's like fire, hot and twisting, taking on new shapes.

And afterward, as we lie there breathless and tender and in awe of what we've done to each other, I wonder what new shapes we'll take on together. Blending and merging, burning brighter. Burning free.

I let her use the shower in my quarters. When she emerges, she is the Mrs. Colding I met all those years ago. Immaculate in her yachtie skirt and polo, her hair done up once more in that severe and gleaming bun, all that silky wildness tucked back into place. She slides in a final bobby pin, smooths her skirt and clasps her hands before her. A chief stew once again. "Ready?"

I nod. "Ready."

The best booze is kept in the saloon. We step into the glass elevator and press the down arrow, making sure we keep ourselves separated. But closer, much closer, than we've previously been in public.

Once or twice, as we descend, the backs of our hands brush against one another. Fleeting, seemingly accidental touches charged with magic.

Nor can we stop ourselves from glancing at each other. I cannot help but grin to myself, and Mrs. Colding betrays her icy exterior with the shadow of a smile.

"How long do you think it will take for Pongshu to black out?" she asks at last.

I shrug. "Seeing as how he has the self-control of a squirrel, I'd say half an hour tops."

Mrs. Colding snorts, and then the elevator is dinging open and we're in the saloon.

During the day, it's spare, clean, almost too sophisticated to be fun. At night, though, it's transformed, becoming an intimate space full of cozy booths and mood lighting. And that light comes from everywhere: the bar, a few portholes aglow with the boat's exterior lighting systems, and the blue LED lights lining the glass-bottomed infinity pool above our heads. That pool light is beguiling, casting wavering neon patterns about us as if we were at the bottom of the ocean. And I hear the pool, too. I hear laughter, splashing, and look up to see a shapely form in a bikini dive into the water. It's Bing. The models have discovered the pool, then.

Bing catches sight of us, waves, and I wave back.

"We're not keeping Pongshu down here, are we?"

Mrs. Colding's question brings me back to myself. "There's the lazaret, where the water toys are kept." I gesture toward a sealed door at the end of the saloon, by the garage where the tenders are propped on their chocks. "Seems fitting." I break off for the bar. I don't bother going around it's half-moon counter—with a grin, I place a hand on the bartop and leap over it.

"Redfearn!" Mrs. Colding snaps, stern worry giving way to laughter.

I land smoothly on my feet on the other side, dust my hands with a wink at Mrs. Colding and peruse the shelves of glowing, backlit bottles. This high I'm riding, this cresting wave of giddiness—it's making me feel invulnerable. I don't even feel the slightest tug of temptation at the sight of all that liquor. It's been completely banished.

"Ah. Bingo." I loft up a bottle, turn to show Mrs. Colding the label printed with Chinese calligraphy. "Rice wine. Pongshu's favorite."

She only watches me, arms crossed, the slightest upturn to her lips.

"What?" I say, laughing as I round the bar.

She shakes her head. "Nothing. It's just—I haven't seen you like this before."

I arch a brow. "Like what?"

She shrugs, eyes soft. "This happy."

This stops me, the bottle held in my hands. We're standing in the middle of the saloon under the pool, bathed in its dreamy blue glow. Somewhere far away, models shriek laughter, splashing water at each other.

"You're sure this will work?" Mrs. Colding goes on finally. "You really think the Steward will go for this trade?"

I drop my eyes, study the bottle. "A father will do anything for his child."

Mrs. Colding stares at me a long beat, wavering blue light catching in her eyes. At last, she steps up to me, brushes a lock of silver hair back from my brow, her voice solemn. "At least this father will."

Our eyes catch, and my chest grows tight. *How?* I think. *How can you see all of me, Mrs. Colding?*

She steps closer, lifting her chin ever so slightly, and lets her lips part. They're pink and supple, delicious-looking. And when her eyes drop for a second—a split second—to my mouth, I know what she's thinking. I'm thinking it, too.

The blood shocks into every part of me, making me flush and grow hard.

We shouldn't be doing this. A crew member could walk in at any moment. We're inviting disaster. Others asking questions. Being found out.

We know better.

Nonetheless, our lips ache closer, almost brushing, the space between us vibrating with tension. We don't speak, as if any word could make us rethink this, could break the spell of the pool's blue light playing over our faces.

Mrs. Colding closes her eyes, ready to lose herself in our kiss.

Thump. Thump. Thump.

The sound is muted, but very, very close. Directly above us, in fact.

When I jerk my head up, what I see makes the skin contract all over my body.

Bing, at the bottom of the pool, staring at us with wide, terrified eyes. She's banging her fist weakly against the glass, bubbles streaming from her mouth in a silent scream as Pongshu sinks his fangs into her neck in a pink cloud of blood.

The world quivers. Black spots dance behind my eyes. Mrs. Colding sucks in a breath and claps a hand to her mouth.

And suddenly, it's no longer Bing at the bottom of that pool, enveloped in clouds of bubbles and blood.

It's Penelope.

Something red explodes at the back of my brain. My hand tightens in a white-knuckled fist around the head of the wine bottle.

Mrs. Colding whirls to me, her face pale as bone. "Redfearn, wait—"

I don't hear her. Because I'm moving. I'm bolting across the saloon, up the winding staircase that takes me abovedeck, not a thought in my head.

When I come upon the aft main deck, it's a scene of chaos. Models are sobbing, some fleeing in terror, tripping over sunbeds, others holding each other as they stare at the pool, shouting at it. Shouting at what's in the pool.

Penelope's—Bing's—body floats to the surface, bobs there head-down in the reddening water, black hair swirling around her.

And then Pongshu is rising out of the shallow end of the pool. He shakes the water out of his pop star hair like a wet dog, his smugness gleaming on him like lotion in the silver moonlight.

"Well," he shrugs, laughing. "Guess I could not a wait after all." He places two delicate talons to his lips. "Oops."

I don't think. I start toward him in a hulking march.

He stops halfway up the pool steps, spreads his arms with a fangsome smirk. "Really? You know you cannot a do anything. You need a me. My father—"

That word obliterates any last thought I had. I flip the bottle in my hand so I'm holding it like a club, bring it smashing down over Pongshu's skull in a shattering of glass.

There's a chorus of shrieks behind me, someone shouting my name, but I'm not listening. All that's very far away. The bottle's impact rocks Pongshu's head back, and I follow him into the pool, wading into the water up to my hips. I'm not done. Righteous vengeance courses through me like a drug, and I succumb to it with radiant joy. I slash down with the jagged stump of the bottle and Pongshu lifts a weak hand. The bottle slices through it, severing one of his taloned fingers, and it plops into the water. But the slash doesn't stop there. It carries through, raking down his face, turning his left eye to jelly. Then I'm grabbing the blood son by his sodden shirt to keep him from falling and I'm ramming the jagged bottle into his neck, over and over, in a rapid series of wet slicing noises until the blood is spraying all over my face and white polo, drenching me red.

It's like dropping a chain. As if years—a lifetime—of all the rage inside me has finally found the outlet it needed. The relief is like a shock of religious ecstasy.

When the bottle finally jams so deep in Pongshu's neck I can't sluck it out again, I wrench it around in an arc and watch, with immense satisfaction, as his head slumps unnaturally back like a deboned fish, his remaining eye still staring at me.

The deck has gone quiet. All I can hear is my heavy breathing, the sound of water lapping over and down the slanted glass wall at the end of the infinity pool in a blood-reddened veil, brimming in a gaudy crimson in the overflow gutter. I blink down at what's before me, the fog of adrenaline clearing, and it takes a moment for me to comprehend that I'm holding onto a corpse. I let it sink back into the water with a mild feeling of disgust. It's happening now. The recognition of what I've done begins to gather around me, pressing in on all sides in a prickling of dull horror and humiliation: *I've destroyed my way of getting Penelope back.*

And standing there to my knees in the pool now turned a deep red, suddenly cold with an ill sweat and with blood freckling my face and beading my lashes, I see that my wavering reflection has turned into a rubber-clad frogman with tactical goggles. That murderous specter of my old self.

I turn around to look behind me.

The remaining models have backed away and are staring at me agape. And there, closer than any of them, her face drained of all color and completely unreadable, is Mrs. Colding.

Our eyes meet.

Shame burns through me, scouring my insides. The world contracts.

And the thought hits me: *Now she's seen you. Now she's seen the real you.*

And immediately following that: *Now you've lost her.*

TWENTY-FIVE
MRS. COLDING

I don't know what I've witnessed. The impact of it is visceral, knocking all the wind out of me. My gorge rises in my throat, and I put a hand to my stomach, grope for a sunbed and sink onto it to keep from vomiting or passing out, or both.

The girl, Bing. Pongshu. Captain Redfearn. The bottle. What he did with the bottle.

Sweat breaks out on my brow. I'm shivering from head to toe. I really think I'm going to faint.

Captain Redfearn is no longer looking at me. He's turned away, the web of one hand mashed against his eyebrows, a gesture of trembling self-loathing. At length he rouses from this, sucks in a deep breath and looks about. Then he remembers the broken bottle in his hand. He tosses it overboard, wades into the blood-reddened pool and grabs what's left of Pongshu and gathers him up in his arms, that pretty head dangling like something filleted, eyes staring at me, and tosses him overboard.

He's covering up what happened.

Yes. That makes sense. Thankfully, it's too late for most of the crew to be up. Most of them have gone to bed. All this has gone on unwitnessed.

Which is good. Because they must have ties with the Steward. Must be paid to give him information.

Which means Captain Redfearn must move quickly before they're seen.

The models are gone, retreated to their quarters, no doubt with doors locked. Their silence will have to be bought. But all this can go away.

Yes. It can. Everything can be all right again.

All this can be forgotten.

I hear weeping. Captain Redfearn is holding Bing's body to him, his big shoulders bouncing up and down as he cradles her against his chest.

Then he throws her overboard with her killer. Pongshu's killer throws her overboard.

Captain Redfearn. A killer.

He sloshes his way out of the pool, and I flinch as he passes me. I hear a button being pressed, see the level of the infinity pool begin to lower. He's draining the pool. Draining the blood. Getting rid of all evidence.

Yes. Yes. Good.

Then water is pooling at my feet. He's standing over me, dripping.

"Come on," he says. "We should get inside before a crewmate sees me like this."

And he offers a dripping hand still stained red with blood.

My response is pure instinct, uncontrollable: I shrink back.

After a beat, Captain Redfearn drops his hand.

I can't meet his eyes. I know I should snap out of this. Say something. Do something. But I can't. Terror is washing over me in great, annihilating waves, and a dim part of me recognizes that I've been triggered. That I should explain this.

I'm sorry. It's okay. It'll pass. I know you're not like him. Not like Mr. Colding.

But in this moment, my body does not know that. It is remembering what Pongshu said in his suite. (*You think you know what he is. But you don't.*) It is screaming with its every last cell to protect itself.

And so the moment passes, and I haven't done anything.

"Okay," Captain Redfearn says, his voice hoarse. Then he is trudging away, wet deck shoes squeaking, and I hear a glass door swing shut.

I put my face in my hands.

Redfearn remains in his quarters all night.

At one point, I knock gently on the door and call his name, ask if he's okay. But he doesn't answer. Even after several more tries.

Eventually, I give up, my insides twisting with guilt and regret, and not a little fear.

I spend the early hours before dawn cleaning the empty pool. I grab a water bucket and a bunch of rags, hop down into the pool, and stiffen all over.

There's a small scattering of blood-caked bottle shards at the bottom of the pool. And at its center, as if on display, a severed finger.

The finger Redfearn severed from Pongshu's hand last night.

I wait through a lurch of nausea and pad up to it.

It's very pale, wrinkled, its stump bloodless, its curved talon impressively long. And it's adorned with a gold signet ring, the initial S stamped onto its face.

I forgot. All blood sons have these signet rings graven with the initials of their blood fathers. Even Adrian kept his, despite turning from Volok long ago. I can remember catching him taking it out at whiles, his face twisting with unknowable passion, before shoving it back into a drawer.

I gather up the bloody shards of glass and toss them into a water bucket, then pick up the finger with a rag, fighting down an urge to gag, and drop it in after.

That done, I take one of the rags and begin to wipe down the pool's red-smeared glass until it squeaks, my head a turmoil of conflicting thoughts.

Did he really have to go that far? Not to mention he didn't think through how this would affect our plans to save his daughter, or our safety.

How can I judge him, though, after what he's been through? Pongshu—a bloody vampire—had just murdered a girl. A girl who probably reminded him of his daughter. How else would he react?

I'm jerked out of this reverie by the sound of thumping music.

My blood turns cold. I kneel there on the laminated glass floor of the pool and cock my ear. Yes. Undeniably music. Party music. Faint but getting closer.

I slowly rise, knees popping and bloody rag in hand, and gaze out through the slanted glass wall at the end of the infinity pool that's overlooking the sea behind.

A 30-foot cruiser yacht is coasting up to the stern of the *Thing*. In the predawn dark it's pulsing with party mood lighting, shifting from red to green to purple, and its bow is packed to the gills with about half a dozen douchey-looking guys who are lofting champagne bottles as they dance and whoop like a bunch of frat boys, wearing nothing but shorts and unbuttoned tropical-print polos.

There's no mistaking it: They're going to board the *Thing*.

My scalp constricts.

And I think: *The bloody rags*. And I think: *Pongshu's damn finger*.

They'd immediately recognize the signet ring.

I snatch the finger out of the bucket and whirl about in a panic. Where to put it?

I think of dumping it in the pocket of my yachtie skirt, but it stinks. They'd smell it on me right away, and I don't trust myself not to gag in front of them.

It has to go overboard.

I fling my arm back, let fly—and slip on a puddle of water at the bottom of the pool.

My aim goes wild. I watch, as in a slow-motion nightmare, as the finger smacks off the boat's glass railing and bounces across the teak deck, coming to rest under a sunbed a good ten feet away.

I gape.

But there's no time to retrieve it. They're already hopping onto the swim deck and stampeding up the stairs to the aft main deck, hooting and hollering.

They're here.

"Helloooo," one of them calls, pulling his sunglasses down his nose as he finds me standing at attention with hands clasped by the pool, waiting for them. "This the reception party?"

And he smiles wide, his mouth flashing with a gold grill on his teeth and fangs.

I sniff in through my nose, lift my chin and give them a once-over. "And who might all of you be?"

Leeches, of course. Sycophants of the Steward's blood son, glomming onto his celebrity like flies on horseshit. They're considerably more cisgender, though: flashy clothes and hair—side swept undercuts, man buns, thick tops with etched lines—and blinged out with heavy gold watches and chains. They make themselves at home as if they've always lived here, and I'm torn between nose-wrinkling disgust and stomach-churning anxiety as they flop onto sunbeds or into chairs, propping their feet up onto tables, their open shirts showing off tatted chests and tubs of bellies.

Asian vampire bros.

And one of them, I notice with a stiffening of my back, lazes on the sunbed hiding Pongshu's finger.

"Pongshu didn't tell you?" the one with the gold grill drawls, a Malaysian by the looks of him. He removes a vape from his mouth to release a smug exhalation of smoke. "He was a little put out having to leave *The Palace of the Fang*. Asked a few of its trust fund babies to rescue him from being bored out of his mind. Even got the degenerate son of the casino owner to come along. Isn't that right, Hong-Li?"

Manbunned Hong-Li gives him the finger. "Fuck you, Feng," he says and begins to deal a deck of cards on a table, turning the aft deck into a gambling den as a buddy pops another champagne bottle, making me jump.

If Redfearn saw this . . .

The Malayasian Feng smirks and leans forward, all suave cockiness, and speaks confidingly from behind a hand. "I'm not like these jerkoffs. Actually an old schoolmate of Pongshu's. You know. The guy who wrote his papers because he couldn't be bothered." He looks me up and down, taking in my long legs, my form-fitting skirt and yachtie polo, and shows a gleam of gold-grilled fang. "I wouldn't have been bored if I was him, though."

My skin chills.

"Heard Pongshu gambled his boat away," Feng goes on, abruptly changing subjects as he looks about at the *Thing* with appreciation. "Hopefully not his signet ring, too. His blood father would fucking kill him."

I choke on a cough.

Another vamp bro has hopped down into the pool and is prowling its length. He stops before the bucket, and my heart slams into my throat as he crouches down, picks up a blood-stained rag between two clawed fingers. "This where the *real* party was at," he admires, turning to me with a grin. "Things get out of hand last night?"

My stomach turns over. "Something like that." I clench my hands and draw myself up, putting on my best chief stewardess voice. "I'm sorry, but Pongshu should have let us know. We would have been prepared for you—"

"Do you smell that?"

The blubbery bro on the sunbed has sat up, champagne bottle in hand, sniffing at the air. His buddies fall silent, nostrils flaring as they scent.

My toes curl into the deck, and I hold my breath.

Then Feng shakes his head. "Fucking Chen. Always smelling something."

I close my eyes, willing myself steady.

"As it is," I go on after a beat, "we cannot take on any more guests at the moment. We're completely full."

"Oh, I think some room can be made," Feng says with an arrogant grin, and leans to the side.

I glance over my shoulder.

It's one of the models. She stands behind the sliding glass door leading inside the dark yacht. She's bleary-eyed, wearing nothing but a skimpy negligee. She cups her hands to the glass door and peers out at us. At all the vamp bros on the aft deck. She stiffens and hurries away again into the darkness.

I turn back to Feng, and find he's right in front of me.

"We won't be long," he promises. Vape smoke curls out of his mouth, swirls seductively around his fangs flashing like a pair of gold daggers in the early morning gloom. "We just want to say hello to Pongshu's new friends. Do we need to ask the captain's permission?"

"No!" I snap, louder than I mean to, images of Redfearn dealing out unholy violence flashing through my mind. I lower my voice with an effort. "No. He's not aboard at the moment. He left me in charge. I can handle this."

"Oooh," the vamp bros coo. "She can handle us!"

Sick, amused laughter.

There's a grating on the teak. Chen has shifted on his sunbed as he looks about, trying to locate the source of the smell.

Sweat is pearling on my upper lip now. I feel the moisture dry up in my mouth.

I can't think. My head has filled with a riotous buzzing as I watch what's unfolding before me. "They're off-limits, I'm afraid," I find myself murmuring, losing my train of thought as Chen scoots off the sunbed so he can lift it up and look beneath. "They belong to the Steward. Do you know—do you know what he'd do if he found out someone stole his property?"

The sunbed scrapes up. Pongshu's signet ring flashes in the shadows, as if wanting to be found.

Chen's face contorts in a dimwitted squint. "What the . . .?"

And I snap.

"Well, then!" I exclaim, clapping my hands, loud enough to startle drunk Chen and make him drop the sunbed over the finger again. I pace free of Feng, gesturing helplessly. "I'm sorry we couldn't accommodate you—"

I jerk up short. Feng, impossibly, is standing in front of me again as if he had always been there. His mouth swells in a golden and terrifying smile. "I'm sure you can find more before you bring Ping-Pong back to daddy." He leans in, his breath rank with rot and the sweet candy smell of vape solution. "Now. Lead the way, sweetheart."

The threat is plain—very plain—in that voice.

The discussion is over.

My back prickles. My eyelids flutter in a slow, involuntary blink.

But I do not look away. I meet his eyes, give him my best, inscrutable chief stew smile. "Of course."

So be it, then.

Feng smirks, steps aside and gestures. "Before the sun rises, if you please."

There is, indeed, a crack of light along the horizon now, reefs of clouds flushing bloodred. Without another glance I saunter across the main deck and along the emptied pool, straight-backed and head held high. Immediately there's the scrape of chairs and sunbeds, the sounds of all of them leaping out of their seats to follow me. I can feel them glancing at each other, full of smug anticipation. Some of them openly snickering. They push each other or bump fists. "Fuck yeah."

They think they've won the lottery.

A great calmness has settled over me. My heartbeat raps at my ribcage, tightening my throat. But I am quite composed, the anxiety well-maintained.

Redfearn doesn't have to deal with this. He doesn't have to do this again. I can take care of this for him.

I can take care of him, in this way.

"Where did you all come from?" I ask, and one could easily—very easily—think it was an innocent question.

Feng only snorts. "Does it matter?"

"Well, we have to make sure you get back safely," I say in a motherly tone.

Hong-Li pipes up. "You think we'd tell Pongshu's blood brother where we were going?" Another snort. "No. We left his morose ass in the Bloodhouse. Came to party with the fun son of the Steward."

So. No one knows where they are.

Perfect.

I sweep through the airy atrium to the glass elevator running through all the decks, picking up a tablet as I go. "Pongshu had quite the night in the saloon downstairs. Hopefully he's awake enough to greet you." I stop before the elevator, swipe open the tablet and tap on an app, and the elevator doors slide open. "Gentlemen first."

Feng smirks as he passes me, and they all cram into the elevator, excited as high school boys at their first swinger party.

I tap the tablet again.

The doors ding closed, and Feng glances down at the arrow that's lit up on the console inside.

It's not the down arrow. It's the up arrow.

His eyes bug. The vape drops from his lips, clattering at his bare feet. "The fuck?" He looks up at the skylight above, and they all look, catching on now.

At the top, the skylight and the glass pavilion up there, open to the outside—it's all turned a glowering red with the reflection of sunrise.

"Whoa, hey," Feng says, lifting his hands and backing away from the console as if it's contagious. Then he jabs a few buttons with his thumb, but they don't respond—because I've locked the elevator. And when they all whirl to me, I'm ascending the floating glass stairs spiraling around the elevator shaft, keeping pace with them as the elevator begins to glide upwards, bearing them with it.

"Hey." Feng bangs his fist against the elevator wall, barely shuddering it under the force. "Hey!" He snarls, a wrathful, fang-baring hiss, then gets himself under control. He inclines his head and points a taloned finger, dropping his voice as if speaking to a child. "Quit the crap. Stop the elevator."

And I keep walking up the stairs. Silent. Staring. Never taking my eyes from them.

Thung-thunk. The glass shudders now. "Fucking bitch! *Fucking bitch!*"

"What the *fuck?*" the other bros shout, putting their hands to their heads.

Then they're all yelling and banging on the walls. But it's no good, even with their unnatural strength. That glass is a quarter inch thick.

And the elevator is creeping closer, closer, to all that light above.

They start losing it now, jumping with their full weight against the glass, kicking with their bare feet. The glass vibrates and frosts in a sudden spiderwebbing of cracks, but holds.

"I'm sorry!" Chen blubbers, getting down on his knees, hands clasped before him as if in prayer. "Please. We're sorry. We'll leave. *Please!*"

They're shouting and cursing and weeping, making the elevator shudder in its shaft, by the time it glides up into the pavilion and the full blast of the rising sun.

Their shrieks make my skin turn to gooseflesh all over my body.

And I tap the tablet, locking the elevator in place in that baking glass pavilion.

It takes a moment for me to catch up. I step up into the pavilion and stop before the locked elevator doors, hold the tablet against my stomach and make myself watch.

They're trying to hide. They have their arms lifted against their faces, but that blast of sun is ripping them apart anyway. It blisters and blackens their flesh, exposing all the red muscle beneath. Some huddle in the corners, trying to delay the inevitable. Feng, on the other hand, doesn't. He staggers to the doors, palms thunking against the glass, talons clicking, and bares his golds at me, eyes cores of murderous rage.

I do not look away. I hold his gaze as the sun burns away his hair and pits his cheeks, withers the gums back from his dental jewelry, turns his eyes bloodshot. I'm still watching as the flames raze his scalp and engulf his body, licking against the glass, obscuring his face in a roaring cocoon of fire. Then his knees crumble out from under him and he drops away, the ash whirling about in that enclosed elevator, drifting gentle as snowflakes onto all those blackened bones and piles of soot. And a fanged gold grill, grinning in the heat.

I turn my face to the sun and watch it rise, dawning on a boat now made safe again. By me. I shut my eyes, soaking in the warmth, the understanding—at last—of what Redfearn felt. The understanding of what is necessary, and what can and can't be helped. The protective and frightening power of violence.

It has never been so clear to me. What he is, and what he is not. The kind of person—the kind of thing—that he is not, and how lucky I am to know such devotion. A humility, an unexpected and breath-stealing gratitude, opens within me, and I feel in myself a new and dutiful love, feel myself newly, and inexhaustibly, resourceful.

I feel safe.

TWENTY-SIX
CAPTAIN REDFEARN

I don't feel safe.

I lock the door to my quarters, dip into the head and flip the faucet on, vigorously scrub the blood off my face until the sink is splashed red with it. I don't recognize that my chest is heaving, that the breath is wheezing in and out of me in angry, despairing snarls, that my eyes are blurring up. I take a look in the mirror and see that there's blood still in my hair, soaking my polo. I need it off. I need to erase all evidence of what I have done. I peel the shirt over my head, unbuckle my belt with shaking hands, strip off everything else and blast myself raw in the shower. Then I'm wringing out my blood-soaked polo in the sink until my hands hurt, using it to wipe down the sink until it's spotless.

I wonder if Mrs. Colding ever cleans like this.

I stuff the shirt into my mouth to stifle the scream, stuff down all that despair inside me, and hear the knock on the door.

I freeze, breath held and dripping naked, in front of the sink.

"Redfearn?"

I can't answer her. I can't let her see me like this. I wait as still and quiet as prey, my heart jumping into my throat and jamming there, until the knocking stops. Footsteps fade away.

She's gone.

I let the shirt slap into the sink and lean against it, my shoulders shaking, my knees weak. Then I'm pacing about the quarters with my hands in my hair, the breath hissing through my clenched teeth. I'm replaying in my head, over and over, the way Mrs. Colding couldn't look at me when I stood before her in my sodden deck shoes, Pongshu's blood still on my face. I feel as if the floor has opened up beneath my feet. As if all sense of stability has been destroyed.

How can she trust me now? How am I to save my daughter now?

This is what I've always been. A fuckup.

I can feel it all coming back. That old sense of humiliation and failure that keeps at your heels like a stray dog, as devoted as a shadow. Invading every corner and crevice of your life, blocking out the light, until you feel that your very existence is a shameful thing.

I flop back on the bed and mash my palms into the cups of my eyes, sucking back a wrenching sob.

Sometime later, and somewhere far away—or as close as in my head—I hear screams. The hair-raising shouts of those whose lives are ending.

Yes. Ending. It's all ending.

I let my hands flop at my sides and stare up at the ceiling, feeling drained, and clear, and filled with a cold, hard certainty.

I know what to do.

TWENTY-SEVEN
MRS. COLDING

In the full light of morning, I knock on the door to Redfearn's quarters.

"Redfearn? Can I come in, please?" When he doesn't respond, I set my jaw and turn the knob, bracing myself to be greeted by an angry response.

But he's not there. The room is empty, the bed unmade.

Everything stretches out before me in nauseating dilation.

Have I made a huge oversight? Maybe I should have never left him alone. Maybe his tendency to be hard on himself goes to deeper, and darker, places than I want to admit to myself.

For a moment, I think of finding another body on this boat, and my mind banishes this image.

No.

Then it comes to me. My head snaps up. I take a harsh breath in through my nose.

I know where he'll be.

I take the spiral stairs enveloping the elevator, my eyes downcast. I take my time, drawing it out. Even when I step off the last step, I don't want to look. I'm afraid he'll be there. I'm afraid he won't be there.

I flutter my eyes up, and the relief washes through me, so overwhelming it makes me lightheaded.

He sits at the bar in the empty saloon, arms crossed on the bartop, chin resting on them, staring at an unopened bottle of Jack Daniels stood before him.

I take in a slow, measured breath, let it out, and walk up to him.

I stop maybe five paces from him. He looks terrible. He's thrown on a new, rumpled polo, its buttons mismatched, and his face is haggard, unshaven, dark circles under his eyes. He looks as if he's been crying.

He doesn't turn to me when I speak. "Can we talk?" When he doesn't stop me, I take a cautious step closer. "I'm sorry I froze last night. I—I was in shock."

His knuckles whiten on the bartop. His teeth clench. "Messed it all up," he hoarses.

My stomach drops. "We can find another way to get Penelope."

This elicits a snort from him, as if I'm not getting it. "Messed *everything* up."

I furrow my brow. "What do you mean?"

His breathing has gotten deeper. He slows his words down, lets them out in short, careful, bitter statements, as if ticking off a list inscribed on his heart. "I failed as a father. I drove away my child. I wrecked my marriage. And now"—his jaw clenches—"and now when I'm finally trying to save my daughter, I—" He chokes up and his chin quivers, tears starting in his eyes. He puts a hand over them.

Then he wipes this away, sniffs in hard through his nose and sits up on the barstool, drags the whiskey bottle toward him.

My heart twists, a swell of sympathy and panic rising in my throat. I lunge forward and put my hands on his forearm. "You're not that man anymore. You've changed. And what you did to Pongshu . . ." I swallow. "That was . . . unfortunate. But it's completely understandable you would act that way."

He hesitates, his big hands gripping the whiskey bottle, one over the other. A great battle waging inside him.

"Please," I whisper, rubbing my thumb on his forearm. "You've come so far. Don't give in now. You don't need that. You're better than that."

These words seem to splash him like acid. He winces against them, his eyes shut, his chest rising slow and deep.

"I think," I say, leaning closer, "I think you're being too hard on yourself. You've mentioned your father before, and I think he taught you that you—that your reaction to his disrespect was the problem. Not his disrespect. And it ended up making it hard for you to regulate your emotions, because they were never validated. You were made to believe they were wrong. And so when you feel like you've done something wrong, your self-criticism is—it's out of proportion."

He's trembling now, as if my words are bringing back a flood of memories. I rub his arm again.

"I know this because—because Mr. Colding made me feel this way, too. And it's not true. You don't have to be ashamed of who you are, Redfearn."

That word—*ashamed*—makes him wince again, as if it cuts to the core of something. He makes a noise in his throat, somewhere between a cough and a growl. Then he abruptly shakes his head, giving in to ruination. He twists off the cap of the whiskey bottle with a brutal wrench and drags a shot glass to him, bends the bottle to pour.

Panic skirls up inside me. I hesitate, debating outcomes, and blurt it out.

"Right before dawn, we had some visitors."

The whiskey bottle freezes over the shot glass.

"Pongshu apparently invited them," I go on, seizing on his attention. "They were going to feed on the models. Maybe even the crew."

He jerks his head at me, gray eyes flashing, and I wet my lips. My mouth is suddenly dry.

"But I . . . took care of them."

His eyebrows bounce up. "What?"

"I locked them in the elevator. In the pavilion, as the sun was rising." I swallow. "They had nowhere to hide."

His face has gone almost scarily pale. He straightens, makes to move toward me.

"I'm okay," I assure him. "It was—I'm okay. I cleaned up what was left. Sunk their boat. It's all taken care of." I meet his eyes. "But when it comes to you, now I know—I know you wouldn't ever be violent toward me."

He cocks his head, unconvinced.

"Yes, you still have work you need to do on yourself," I qualify with a tender smile. "We all do. And once we're back on land, you're going to get a bucket load of therapy to learn how to control those emotions of yours."

He opens his mouth as if to object, and I stop him with a raised finger.

"But that doesn't mean you're not a good person, or that this can't work." I slip my hand into his, duck my head to catch his eye. "I *want* this to work."

He searches my eyes, moving his back and forth. "I didn't scare you off?" he asks, and the hope in his voice breaks my heart. "I know that everything you went through with Mr. Colding, it left you—and I don't want you thinking I'm—" He breaks off and glances up at the squeaky-clean glass bottom of the infinity pool above us. No doubt remembering Bing floating in a cloud of blood. What he did after. He jerks his eyes away again. "After last night, I don't want you thinking I'm anything like—"

I shake my head, trying to communicate all my love for him with my eyes as I slip my fingers around the whiskey bottle, gently free it from his grip so I can set it on the bartop and hold both his hands in mine. "No. I don't."

He blinks at me, his lips quivering, halfway to a smile. But he's not done. "You're not afraid of me?"

I part my lips, taking a moment to consider my words—and that's more than enough hesitation for him.

"Thanks for speaking with me," he gruffs, and my heart lurches as he gently slides his hands out of mine. "I appreciate it."

"Redfearn . . ."

"I'm sorry," he says, turning his face away as he prepares to stand. "I just—I need time to think. I need to figure out our next steps." He stops, considering the deck. "Who did you say those vamps were again?"

"Friends of Pongshu's," I repeat, feeling sluggish and dull. "Some of them were friends of his blood brother, I guess."

Redfearn stills all over. "The Steward has another blood son?"

A vague feeling of import hits me now. "Yes. He does."

"Where is he?"

"Someone mentioned a place called the Bloodhouse—"

The captain's off his stool before I finish my sentence, an iron purpose in his step again. I hurry after him, spluttering. "Hang on. What—what does that mean?"

Redfearn stops and turns so suddenly I almost bump into him. "It means we still have a chance."

"What do you—"

"We're going to kidnap the Steward's other blood son," he announces, a spark of that old rakishness coming back into his face, "and trade him for my daughter."

CAPTAIN'S LOG

Mainland Coast to Bloodtown, December 11th.
Ship: *Thing*.
Speed: 25 knots.
Distance: 33 mi.
Weather: Overcast day.
Notes: Models dropped off on land with money to return home. Also to buy their silence. A relief to have them safely out of the way before continuing on.

Back on track.

TWENTY-EIGHT
CAPTAIN REDFEARN

It takes all day to find the entrance to the river leading up into Bloodtown.

Adrian had told me its location, long ago. Pointed at a place on a chart west of the *The Palace of the Fang* and upriver from the coast, where I'd scratched out an "X" and left it at that. But there are a lot of fucking river estuaries lining the southern coast of China.

It's nearing dusk, clouds rolling in and shutting out the light, when we find it.

The river is maybe ten meters wide, and spanning it is the biggest arch I've ever seen. It's a paifang, a traditional Chinese gateway with multi-tiered roofs upheld by massive posts painted a deep red. Probably forty meters tall, it soars high enough to allow passage even for a superyacht, and is decorated with dragons, wolves, bats, gilt Chinese calligraphy glinting in the failing light. An immense hulk of a thing that's fallen into disrepair over the years, giving it a haunted look. Its roofs sag, its red beams and ramshackle shingles streaked white with birdshit. And beyond it, deep, eerie water winds between dark green mountains, lined with Chinese lanterns glowing like fireflies.

"Does that say what I think it says?" I ask Mrs. Colding beside me at the bow, jutting my chin at the giant gold characters stamped into the face of the gateway.

Mrs. Colding nods. "We're here."

Using the yacht controller, I carefully guide the *Thing* under the gate. That span passes over us, its gargantuan underside blotting out the sun and casting us in shadow. Bats hiss in hanging colonies and swoop away, teeth clicking. Then we're gliding up the river gorge that's barely wide enough for our boat, flickering lanterns passing us on either side.

Behind us, the glowering light of sunset slips away, and a stealing cold sets in. Delicate mists creep out on the water, laying claim to the river.

Night has fallen.

I shift my weight, harrumphing deep in my throat. I'm not sure how to act around Mrs. Colding right now. I feel as if I've been thrown back to how it was before we disclosed our feelings for each other: unsure of my footing, and embarrassed to boot. I can't shake the sense that I've made a fool of myself. That I've broken something.

Mrs. Colding senses this. She moves closer and slips her arm through mine, lays her head on my shoulder.

She's never done this before. It closes up the breath in my throat.

"I love you," she whispers.

My chest tightens. My throat clicks as I swallow. "I love you, too," I croak back.

"You think this will really work?"

I grunt. "It has to. I don't know what else could. We don't know anything about this base, how to get into it, how to find Penelope. The only thing we can do is make a bargain, hope the Steward loves this other blood son just as much."

"A bargain," Mrs. Colding repeats to herself. "So we have to gamble."

I snort. "I guess so."

She lifts her head, stands slightly on tiptoe, and kisses my cheek.

That touch is still spreading warmth through me by the time we round a bend in the river and see Bloodtown.

It's a water town. A gathering of stone and wood houses built on the river that seems summoned up from the ancient past. Canals thread through it, some of them spanned by high-arching bridges. Sampans and barges float, moored, in the mists at the bottom of stone steps descending into the water. And while the eaves of the riverside houses are hung with Chinese lanterns, flickering like will-o'-the-wisps in some unreliable vision, it is as deserted as a graveyard. Most of its houses are dark, as rundown and haunted-looking as the paifang. Their plaster stained by time and monsoons. Their shingles crooked. Their roofs sunken.

"What is this place?" Mrs. Colding asks in a hushed voice.

I cagily eye the passing canals, the empty windows, my voice grim. "It's where their addicts come to die."

"Addicts?"

"Those who become addicted to feeding and can't stop. They're . . . drunks, essentially."

Mrs. Colding glances at me, and I shift uncomfortably. "As one of them, if you go too far with your feeding, your body becomes corrupted. They . . . drink themselves to death."

I can feel Mrs. Colding's eyes on me, but cannot look at her. My ears grow hot. I lift my chin and harrumph deep in my throat. "They call it Bloodtown because of its blood bar. The Bloodhouse, they call it."

"A blood bar," Mrs. Colding echoes, shivering. "Where is it?"

I jut my chin. And when she looks ahead, her breath catches.

We've reached the far end of Bloodtown. The houses give way to a wide, swampy lake dotted with red-blossomed lotuses at its muddy edges. And jutting up from that lake is a tower of a house ablaze with light. It has nine floors, each one concentrically smaller than the last, each with roofs curved up sharply at the corners like fangs. Windows glow from every floor, outshining all of Bloodtown, and all of it is carved with intricate undulating bargeboards painted red. A creepy, ornate relic surrounded by a small fleet of superyachts at anchor in the mists shrouding the lake.

Fuck, it looks even more awful than I thought it would.

I turn to Mrs. Colding, bracing myself. "I want you to—"

"Before you say anything, I'm going with you." She holds up a hand before I can get worked up. "*The Palace of the Fang* was one thing. But this is a bar. And I know how close to the edge you are right now. You'll need support in there. And after that little cremation incident with the elevator, I think you know I can handle myself."

"I know you can handle yourself," I begin, a little beleaguered. "I just—a place like that, I'm worried your PTSD—"

"I'll be fine."

I sigh. "Mrs. Colding—" I try again, rather half-heartedly.

"I'll meet you in the tender," she snips and sweeps away.

For a moment, I want to be angry. I really do. But I can't ignore the rush of relief—and gratitude. The gratefulness for not having to be alone right now.

I'm smiling as I tap the button to drop anchor.

TWENTY-NINE
MRS. COLDING

Maybe it's not as bad as I think, I wonder as our tender approaches the Bloodhouse of Bloodtown.

I glance at Captain Redfearn at the helm, at his stern gray eyes taking in the great height of the tavern before us. I don't know where I stand with him now. I don't know what happened to us. Trying to sort it out in my head is tearing me up inside, making me mourn what was lost, and I have to remind myself to just hold on and wait it out, be the support he needs. Things can change.

Maybe he can get over this stumble. Maybe he'll stop beating himself up about Pongshu.

Maybe we'll be okay.

Then we're nosing up alongside the other tenders moored at the Bloodhouse's rotting dock, and I don't have any more room for these thoughts.

I have plenty of other things to worry about at present.

I jump out with the bow line in one hand, a pair of high heels in the other. I tie us off and hop on one foot to slip on a heel, glance at the other superyachts moored on the lake. Some dark, others lit. Some with people on deck, forlorn figures in the shifting gray fog, their glowing eyes on me making me shiver. There's probably at least a dozen of those white boats.

That's a lot of bloodsucking guests waiting inside that bar.

Then Redfearn's at my side and we're looking at each other, our hands clasping, gripping tight.

"Ready?" he asks.

I nod, not trusting myself to speak, and he touches my cheek. Everything inside me aches, cherishing that touch and what it means. *Don't go*, I say to myself.

Then he's pushing at the huge, red iron-studded door before us, and we enter the Bloodhouse of Bloodtown.

It's a shambles straight out of my nightmares. Rotting wood posts, stained flagstones covered in damp crimson rugs, an age of glory and decadence still clinging to it all like a foul miasma. Chinese lanterns hang in the gloom, coated in dust and pulsing like red-hot dragon eggs, lighting a hexagonal space full of empty drinking tables. And dominating everything is a bar, its back counter piled high with dusty bottles of dubious scarlet liquid, some with corpse candles stoppered in their spouts. The candleflames gutter and drip beards of wax as the door shuts behind us.

My flesh crawls. My gorge rises in my throat. I want to flee. Every stewardess instinct in me is screaming so loudly that I do not notice at first that there's a woman behind the counter. Short, seamed in wrinkles, her opulent qipao as ancient as herself.

The mama-san.

She beckons a wizened claw, and we approach.

"You here first time," she croons, tapping the lined skin beneath one eye with a yellow talon. "I remember all."

Behind her, roaches clamber over the liquor bottles in little ticking noises, perch on pour spouts and flutter their wings delicately, some mounted atop each other. They're mating.

A primordial revulsion stirs in me, and I shiver.

Somewhere, I hear a dripping sound.

"I Madam Zhao," the mama-san announces in a sly voice. "Welcome to Bloodhouse." She bends her back in a stiff bow, eyes clouded with cataracts rolling up to peer at us. "Why warmbloods here?"

Redfearn clears his throat. "We're here to see Pongshu's brother."

"Ah." The old crone's mouth widens in a shifting of wrinkles, revealing one yellowed fang and one cracked and splintered down to a rotting stub. "The brother."

I'm not listening, though; something has caught my eye. It's the walls. They're *moving*. I take a step closer, feeling an icy foreboding gather in my gut. There's something running down them. Dark red, trickling in rivulets down the old grain. Something bats at my eye, and when I brush at it, the pads of my fingertips gleam red in the gloom.

Blood.

I lift my eyes, very slowly, and see, on the ceiling above me, blood gathering in the cracks between the boards, pluming into drops and falling.

The dripping everywhere is blood.

And it hits me now in a gust of corruption, making my eyes water: the stench of spoiled meat, the snarling of slaughterhouse flies.

"Jiangshi here," Madam Zhao says, and points a curved yellow talon upward. "At top."

And drifting toward the middle of the tower, Redfearn and I crane our heads and see that a shaft runs down though eight floors of the Bloodhouse in stomach-turning vertigo, encircled by a rickety wooden staircase. And from the ninth floor, a constant rainfall of blood drips down through that shaft. It oozes down the walls, soaks into the rugs and fills up the crevices between the flagstones, so that it seems the very house itself is bleeding.

Somewhere, I hear a faint scream echoing in that tower. The ticking of roaches and buzzing of flies reaches a deafening pitch in my ears. I latch onto Redfearn's hand again, my stomach giving a warning flop. It takes everything in me to not throw up.

The mama-san is laughing a raspy, hacking laugh as we ascend the stairs.

I take my time. The wooden steps creak under our weight and my ankles wobble in my heels, but I don't take them off, don't put a free hand on the sticky banister for balance. The very thought of any bare part of me touching this place makes me feel ill.

I shut my eyes. I don't know how much longer I can stand this. My whole body itches. I feel as if I'm breaking out in hives. Like if I don't scratch this feeling off my skin, I might go mad.

I might even welcome it.

After a while, I must block out what I'm seeing, because I don't remember much on that staircase. I remember passing floors lined with rooms closed off by sliding screen doors, muffled grunts and blurs of flesh behind them. I remember glimpsing a man kneeling naked in a room, head flung back and arms spread as if in prayer; an iron lattice slat opens in the ceiling above and he's drenched in a deluge of blood.

And with every turn of the staircase, we get closer and closer to that ninth floor with its floorboards clogged red and dripping blood down through that dizzying shaft.

I don't want to think about where all that's coming from.

By the time we get to the last few turns of the stairs, I'm leaning against Redfearn, head held high but knees weak and shaking, his arm around me. But there's no going back now.

The stairs creak. Redfearn looks at me on the landing as if asking if I'm ready.

I'm not. I nod yes.

And we step through hanging bead curtains into what's at the top of the Bloodhouse.

I have to blink a moment to take it in. It looks like an opium den. Dimly lit, though not by the kerosene fixtures of the past: a purple neon dragon on the wall, candles wavering in dingy glass holders, all of it red and womblike and oppressive, with only a few moon-shaped windows open to the moonlit night. And in the middle of the room where the addicts are slumped in satiation, long metal straws in their laps like opium pipes, is the source of all that dripping blood.

Everything inside me quails.

It's a fountain heaped with the bodies of women. Here and there black tangles of hair, a staring eye. The ghost-white curves of hips and shoulders and breasts poking out of the crimson lake of blood filling up that pool and overflowing its sides, dripping onto the floorboards, between the cracks, down into the Bloodhouse below. Its spout bubbles up gore in a silence that's otherwise broken only by the drowsy buzz of flies.

And as we near the fountain, I catch sight of a face amongst that crush of bodies. A very familiar face. It opens its eyes, and Evangeline Voper stares at me, a hint of fangs showing as her lips seam back in a sly and knowing smirk.

I slam my lids shut, the scars on my neck throbbing in a painful and familiar way. I can feel those lovely fangs sliding into my neck again, hear her sigh of release. I can't bear it. My breathing gets high and tight in my chest. My heart beats so hard my shoulders shake. I am certain I can hear a slithering, Evangeline Voper rising slinky and mocking out of that mass grave, her naked body smeared head to toe in gore, and I am seized by an almost uncontrollable urge to turn around, run back down those treacherous stairs, an almost hysterical terror possessing me just like it did when I saw that face in its dozens push out of that surreal white shrink wrap in Hibernacula.

How could I be such a fool, my mind thinks all of its own. *It's Hibernacula all over again. Redfearn was right. We've made a mistake. We shouldn't have come here. I haven't processed this yet.*

I'm not strong enough yet.

I swear I can hear footsteps. Evangeline stepping down out of that pool, her dainty bare feet leaving grisly prints behind her as she approaches.

And then, stronger than before: *No. You need to be here. Redfearn needs you. She's just a hallucination, after all. It's just your trauma. You can push through this.*

You have to push through this.

And just when I think I've gotten ahold of myself, there's a sucking sound, a luxurious sigh, and when I open my eyes Evangeline is nowhere to be seen. Only an addict sinking back onto the floor, the tip of his metal straw dripping red. He wipes at his mouth and catches sight of us. Smiles.

"Ah, Madam Zhao say you come for me," he slurs, and lifts his straw in offering. "Care for drink?"

THIRTY
CAPTAIN REDFEARN

I can't stop worrying about Mrs. Colding.

We retire to a private alcove to talk with Jiangshi. It's much too cozy, a small round booth draped in mosquito netting as dusty as cobwebs. And while that curtain at least blurs out the horrors around us, casting us in an intimate, candle-lit gloom, it does nothing to distract me from the fact that Mrs. Colding is going through a traumatic episode much like in Hibernacula.

I don't know what's going on in her head, but I can guess. By the way she won't look at that fucking fountain, yeah, I have a pretty damn good idea.

What the fuck was I thinking, letting her convince me to take her with me?

I try not to keep glancing at her. She has her hands folded neatly in her lap, and I can see the fear and revulsion radiating off her. When that frayed and filthy mosquito netting brushes against her, she flinches, nostrils flaring, and I know she wants to climb out of her skin.

And yet, despite all this—despite this cascade of trauma that's making her tremble and white-knuckle her hands—she's still here with me. That's how much she loves me.

I slip my hand into one of hers under the table, grip it tight.

Don't worry. I'm going to get this over with.

Jiangshi is not like his blood brother. At all. Whereas Pongshu was flamboyant and slyly gregarious, Jiangshi is wrapped in solemn garments, a mood that's at turns painfully shy, painfully hopeful, blurred with the red-eyed lethargy of a junkie. And he is shaking. He shivers and twitches as if taken with fever, and what's oozing out of his pores is not the sweat of an alcoholic.

It's blood.

He's so bloated with it that he's sweating it out of his body.

Disgust and pity coil together in my gut. Is that what I looked like when I was a drunk? Did others feel about me the way I'm feeling now?

Jiangshi can't sit still, can't help himself. He reaches a trembling hand to open the spigot of an absinthe fountain filled with blood, and a fat bead gathers and splashes red onto the pristine whiteness of a sugar cube laid on a slotted spoon. Drop by drop, the sugar softens and dissolves into the glass of wormwood-green spirits below. When this curious process has turned the glass a deep burgundy, Jiangshi sets the spoon aside with a clatter and takes a greedy swallow. Then he glances at me, his lean, miserable face pinching in a frown. "You must drink."

He snaps his fingers, and a woman with painted cheeks and a tiny miniskirt detaches from the shadows, approaches our table to present a tray of crimson-tinted drinks.

My heart drops.

"No," I croak, flying a sidelong glance at Mrs. Colding. "I can't—"

Jiangshi waves a dismissive hand. "We have drink for warmbloods, too."

"It's not that. I—"

"You will no drink with me?" The hurt in Jiangshi's voice is clear as day, almost childish. Then his eyes hood over. "I only speak with those who drink with me." He leans forward, all geniality gone. "You want talk?" He gestures at the tray. "Drink."

I swallow, feeling cornered and panicky, and glance at Mrs. Colding. The trembling appears to have passed, and she is looking at me, her face full of aching sympathy. And also fear. For me.

I look up at the waitress. "Whiskey, please."

"Red wine," Mrs. Colding murmurs, her voice hollow.

The woman sets down two glasses and melts back into the shadows.

I stare down into mine. Blood swirls in delicate eddies amongst the ice cubes. Mrs. Colding's wine is very, very red.

Jiangshi lifts his blood absinthe, his weeping face aglow with the fever of camaraderie. "To new friends."

Mrs. Colding slowly lifts her glass, takes a ladylike sip and winces a smile. Then she turns to me.

I do not move. I can feel Jiangshi's gaze on me. My heart pistoning in my chest. My hands are sweating, so I rub them on my thighs before I pick up the glass, surprised at my steadiness. I can smell the rich spicy oakiness of the whiskey, can already taste it on my tongue. My mouth, to my shame, begins to water.

I do not look at Mrs. Colding. I feel as if I am acting out a betrayal in front of her.

Jiangshi's eyes glow, watching me.

For you, Pen, I think, and lift the glass to my lips.

The scorching beauty of it sets fire to my mouth, blazing down my throat, into my belly, hot as sin. It's almost dizzying. The joy and terror of it.

And I think, *Ah, yes. There you are again.*

I set the glass back down, restrain myself from pushing it away from me.

Jiangshi smiles. "So what bring warmbloods to Bloodhouse of Bloodtown?" he asks and slumps, sated for now, into the alcove's tufted button upholstery.

It takes a moment to gather my thoughts. I'm beside myself. I feel a bewildering pressure of tears.

Shaking this off, I link my hands on the table and lean forward. "We're here to take you to your blood father."

Jiangshi goes very still. "My blood father ask for me?"

Fighting to keep all deceit and guilt out of my face, I nod.

The blood son still has his metal straw with him; it looks like a steel wand. He takes it up, taps it pensively against his shoulder like a bored field marshal with a baton. "Why?"

"He—" I share a conflicted look with Mrs. Colding. "He said he misses you."

"He did?"

Another nod.

Jiangshi sits there staring at us, his expression inscrutable. I feel my hands start to sweat again, wonder what's going to happen next here.

Then Jiangshi's face breaks into a huge grin. "My blood father want to see me."

Mrs. Colding and I glance at each other, smiling tentatively. "Yes."

"My blood father want to see me!" Jiangshi lifts his blood absinthe, laughing, and we lift ours in answer, laughing uneasily along with him.

Jiangshi knocks his absinthe back, and I know we need to join in. After a quick sip, I try to put my whiskey down, but Jiangshi cups his hand under my glass, tips it back up. "Drink! Drink!" he crows.

Spluttering, I choke the whole glass down, clop it on the table to Jiangshi's cheers, eyes watering and overtaken by a sudden flash of anger, a feeling of having been taken advantage of. This, in turn, is followed by a feeling of irrevocable compromise, wild and anxious and ferociously pleasurable.

But Mrs. Colding has gripped my arm under the table, and I turn to her. She's staring at me, eyes shining. She's almost smiling. In sympathy, and clear concern, but also pride.

We did it. He's going along with it.

We're going to get my daughter back.

I beam at her.

Jiangshi is oblivious to all of this. He twirls a sharp finger in the air. "Another round!"

Mrs. Colding edges me another look, this one more wary, and drops her voice into a courteous yacht stew tone. "You are very gracious, but—"

"Thought he would ask Pongshu," the blood son murmurs to himself. "He always love Pongshu best. Pongshu like him. Share taste for cruelty." He looks down at his hands, at a gold signet ring on his finger bearing the Steward's initial, and his lips thin.

Mrs. Colding and I share a look, unsure what to do with this sudden turn in mood.

I lean forward, my voice gentle. "If we want to make Volok's base by tonight, we should—"

"My father, my real father," Jiangshi continues, not listening, "he disown me. When I get a turned, I no longer age. My family not know what wrong with me. Call me demon. Renounce me. Spit in my face. Father throw me into street." His lip trembles, his eyes growing glassy. "So Steward became my father. I give him all my love. But was never enough for him. I not like Pongshu. Not willing to hurt like they hurt. So Steward hurt me." Jiangshi lets out a strange, strangled laugh. "Maybe I cursed."

Mrs. Colding swallows and looks at me, but I can't return her gaze. A familiar weight is starting to press down on my chest as I listen, my breathing getting deeper, faster, that word knocking in my ears: *cursed*.

"So I come here," Jiangshi goes on, wiping at his eyes. "So I can forget." He dips his straw into his macabre absinthe and takes a last draw, slumps back into his seat again, a sleepy smile on his face despite his shivers and blood sweat. "But maybe Father change. Maybe he love me again." He shuts his eyes.

Years and years ago, an eight-year-old Penelope watches me from the hallway as I open the front door. *Why you leaving, Daddy?*

I shoot up out of my seat and stumble through the mosquito netting, a hand to my brow. A burning agitation is making me pace, my chest heaving. I can't breathe.

Mrs. Colding, sliding out of the alcove after me, takes me by the arm and gently leads me away from Jiangshi. "What is it?" she asks in a low voice, glancing at the somnolent addicts around us.

"I don't—I don't know if I can do this," I get out, and glance at Jiangshi pitifully slumped in the alcove. "He may be one of them, but he doesn't deserve this."

Mrs. Colding stills. "What are you saying?"

I take in a deep breath, try to slow the hammering of my heart. "I'm saying I don't know if I could live with myself if we bring him to the Steward. The Steward might not even want him. It would destroy him."

Mrs. Colding's eyes flutter at this. She also glances back at Jiangshi, chewing her lip. "What do we do, then?"

I shrug. "Be honest and tell him. Find another way."

"You sure? That's a big risk."

We both stare at him. "I know. But I can't think of any other way. We'll just have to trust he doesn't tell anyone."

Mrs. Colding looks at me now, searching my eyes, and nods. "Okay."

Jiangshi jolts when I rouse him with a hand on his shoulder. "Father?" he mutters.

I crouch down so I'm on a level with him. "Hey. I have to tell you something, Jiangshi."

The blood son looks around blearily, reaches for his blood absinthe, sees it's empty and pushes it away with a grimace. "Where that girl," he mumbles.

"Jiangshi. I can't take you to the Steward."

The blood son blinks at me, eyes clearing now. "What?"

"I'm sorry," I say, glancing at Mrs. Colding watching with hands clasped tightly in front of her. "But I lied. The Steward didn't ask for you. I made that up because—because I wanted to get my daughter back, and I was hoping he'd let her go if I brought you to him."

Jiangshi stares at me a long moment, pulls himself up in the booth. "You lie to me?"

"I know," I say, dropping my head. "I shouldn't have. I feel like an asshole. And now that I know about you and your blood father—" I break off, not knowing what to say.

Then Mrs. Colding's hand is on my shoulder, squeezing. *You know what to do.*

"I had a father like yours," I go on, fighting to keep my voice from wavering. "And I know—I know how much it hurts to know your father doesn't love you. So I'm choosing to be honest with you."

Jiangshi face twitches, as if he's been slapped. He bites the inside of his lip. His eyes fill.

"You deserve better than him, Jiangshi. You deserve to have people in your life who love you for who you are." I squeeze his shoulder. Hard. "There is nothing wrong with you. You did nothing to merit him treating you the way he did."

Jiangshi's cheeks gleam. He looks down at the metal straw in his hands, and tears fall into his lap.

"I hope you find a way to love yourself again."

Then I'm standing before I can't make myself do so, a lightness in my heart that hasn't been there in a long time, and Mrs. Colding is looking at me with such pride I don't know what to do with this feeling.

I take her hand in mine. "Let's go," I tell her.

But when we start for the stairs, we come up short. Because a figure is blocking our way. One of the blood addicts has risen from the floor. Perhaps he was never an addict, as I don't see any of those tiny droplets of blood weeping from the pores of his skin. Perhaps he was listening to us the entire time.

He wears black traditional Chinese clothing, and he is smiling.

"Did you really think there was only one bounty hunter after you, Captain Redfearn?" he purrs in a silky voice, and there's a stirring behind him.

All around us, all the remaining addicts are rising from the floor.

The bounty hunter spreads his taloned hands, fangs glinting. "All due respect to Mr. Lelouch, but sometimes it takes our kind to get things done."

THIRTY-ONE

MRS. COLDING

All the pride I'm feeling for Captain Redfearn is instantly replaced with sinking dread.

The patrons of the Bloodhouse close in, eyes glowing in the dimness of the lounge, teeth flashing. They rise from the floor, the alcoves, leaving their metal straws behind, trailing toward us in a mindless horde of the undead. They all but drool with a thirst for the blood of the living.

Their fangs flash, making the scars on my neck throb again, and a shudder skitters down my spine.

I can feel it. The trauma. It's creeping back in, starting the shaking again, fraying at my nerves and scattering my thoughts, turning my mind into a numb blank that does not have to be here, does not have to witness this.

This is survival.

Redfearn moves slightly in front of me and backs us away, one hand held out in a gesture of conciliation. "Whatever the bounty is, I'll double it. Just let us go."

The bounty hunter shakes his head, a look of pity in his eyes. "A warmblood like you wouldn't get it, would you?" He juts his chin forward, fangs bared. "Nothing can compete with the Commodore's favor."

Redfearn shakes his head, eyes pleading. "Please. I don't want violence."

There's a wicked gleam of teeth in response. A promise.

There will be violence.

Talons flash. I let out a yip of a scream and fly a hand to my mouth. With a grunt, Redfearn goes down to one knee, his left temple wet with three nasty slashes.

All the addicts stare as blood drips onto the floor.

Adrenaline courses through me, heady and nauseating, telling me to flee, to escape. How did we get here? How is everything unraveling?

The bounty hunter steps forward in a creaking of floorboards, looming over Redfearn. A herald of death.

And I notice, with a pulse of blood in my ears, that Redfearn's hand is dipping behind his back to where a pistol is jammed into the waistband of his khaki shorts. The Glock he confiscated from that other bounty hunter.

Do it, I silently beseech him. *Please.*

And he hesitates, a flush rising hotly up his neck.

No. It's okay. There's nothing wrong with resorting to that in this moment.

You can show that side of you.

But he can't seem to break out of it. His hand trembles, not touching, and not pulling away from, the grip of the gun.

A smirk creeps up the bounty hunter's face, and he lifts his arm. Elongated talons gleam like shears.

Somewhere in this accursed tower, I hear Evangeline Voper's laughter.

And I think, *Fuck you, trauma.*

I dart forward, snatch the Glock out of Redfearn's waistband and lift it and—

Schwick!

The bounty hunter stares, Jiangshi's metal straw buried almost to its end in his left ear canal. He topples, the floorboards jumping, and the blood son stares down at the killer's body, almost too stunned to believe what he's done. He looks at us.

"Go," he snaps. "*Now!*"

I don't think. I dive for Redfearn, grab his arm and yank him up—

But Redfearn is jerking me short, reaching out a hand. "*No!*"

Because a body is flying past us. It's Jiangshi. The snarling patrons of the Bloodhouse have picked him up and flung him through the air, and he's crashing through a window in a brilliant comet's tail of shattered glass, sailing out into the night.

Redfearn rushes to the broken window on his knees, pokes his head out into the whistling night wind and looks down with me over his shoulder.

Jiangshi lies impaled on one of those horned corners of the roof below, blood coughed up onto his face, his eyes reflecting twin moons.

Redfearn pushes himself back onto his ass and away from that sight. His face has turned the frightening color of ash.

And behind us, the Bloodhouse patrons glide closer with grinning mouths.

I tremble all over.

I need to make a decision. Now. I need to keep ahead of this incapacitating shock and do this for Redfearn, as I did with Feng and his crew. I know what he's in the grip of, what's making him falter.

I need to decide for both of us.

"Get on your feet, Redfearn."

The yacht captain blinks, as if coming back from somewhere very far away. "What?"

I dip to slip off one heel, then the other. "I said get on your feet."

Redfearn blinks, looks at the Glock I've trained with both hands on the grinning horrors advancing on us, and seems to remember himself. He staggers up.

I arch a brow at him. "Ready?"

He stares at me. Then at the horde of blood addicts blocking our way back down the Bloodhouse. Behind us at the broken window and the water far, far below.

"Ready?" I say again, and when Redfearn turns back to me, he gets it.

He nods.

The pale things in that room lunge toward us, but we've already turned and leapt out of the broken window into the night.

Cold air whistles in my ears. I glimpse moonlit water, the white gleam of yacht hulls, the firefly lights of Bloodtown in the distance, and pray we've jumped far enough to clear the descending roofs below and avoid Jiangshi's fate.

Then the water is rushing up toward my bare feet, and I think, *Let it be deep enough*.

The impact is crushing, violently cold. For a moment, all is darkness, a chaos of bubbles, and then I'm kicking, surging up, and up, until my head breaks the surface and I gasp in air again.

I whirl about. Redfearn is beside me, unharmed, and relief jumps into my throat. I've managed to hold onto the Glock as well.

Then there's a series of splashes behind us. Things dropping from above.

They're following us.

My body goes ice cold. I turn to Redfearn, the same expression on both our faces.

We start swimming madly for *The Thing*. She's only twenty paces away, but those things behind us are blindingly fast. One glance behind and I see them gliding through the water like sharks.

We're not going to make it.

We come abreast of the boat's starboard hull, but it's still another thirty meters to her stern. They'll catch up to us by then.

There's nothing to do. It's over.

Despair descends on me, heavy as the crushing pressure of the deep sea. I don't want this to be my final moments. I don't want to die here in this swampy water abuzz with mosquitoes, sucked under with my love. Nor do I want to resort to the Glock clutched in my hand. Put it to my own head.

I whirl about, looking for Redfearn. *Please. I need you right now. I need you to shake yourself out of it—*

"Cover your ears."

Redfearn is ahead of me, holding up the yacht controller. He must have had it in his pocket the whole time.

"What?"

"Cover your ears!" he shouts again, and points upward.

There's something on the bow I've never noticed before. Some kind of acoustic device that looks like a satellite dish, facing outward. A sound cannon. An anti-piracy system.

I clap my hands over my ears, the relief dumping into me, and Redfearn presses a button on the yacht controller.

Even with that layer of protection, I can hear it. An excruciating, eardrum-splitting decibel of punishing sound. It's like the piercing ring of a thousand high-tension lines, a hellish microphone feedback whine. It beams out across the water behind us, ruffling the surface of the lake into a path of overlapping concentric ripples, and the things following us shriek and howl and clutch their bleeding ears, some of them diving under to avoid that sonic blast. A moment later, the silvery bodies of stunned fish bob to the surface, mouths gaping and round eyes staring.

That should buy us some time.

"Come on!" Redfearn shouts, pressing another button, and the *Thing*'s anchor clanks up out of the lake and into its hawsepipe as we plunge forward again.

I'm so proud of you, Redfearn.

By the time we're nearing the stern, only a few determined patrons of the Bloodhouse are still after us. I can see their glowing eyes, the murderous glint of their teeth, like moray eels. It saps all the strength out of me.

"Come on," Redfearn urges, hauling himself onto the swim deck. I toss the Glock onto the deck after him and try to follow, but I'm so exhausted I can't make it. I sink back into the water.

"Redfearn," I wheeze, the panic tight in my voice.

I can hear the splashing of those things nearing us. They're about to round the stern.

"Redfearn!"

The captain spins on his knees and grabs my outflung arms, the veins standing out on his face as he heaves me up out of the water—

Just as those things burst out of the lake behind me like a shoal of sharks, clawed hands swiping at my bare legs, fangs snapping.

"*Fucking Christ!*" I screech, clinging to Redfearn.

And Redfearn straightens, the yacht controller in his hands.

"Get the fuck off my woman," he growls, and pushes a pair of knobs up to full-throttle.

There's a deep hum beneath our feet, the bronze blades of the *Thing*'s stern propellers whirring to hungry life, and the fanged terrors are sucked under. In a moment, the churning foam at the *Thing*'s stern turns red and thick with chopped-up chum.

Propped on my elbows on the swim deck, gasping and soaked to the bone, I'm overwhelmed by a heady confusion of awe and arousal.

Redfearn grabs my arm. "Let's go."

We pad down teak gangways, throwing glances behind us. The other yachts are already coming to life, lights flicking on, anchors rattling up, thrusters boiling froth as they turn about in pursuit.

"Fuck," Redfearn hisses. He's working the joystick of the yacht controller as he runs, swinging the bow of the *Thing* about. Curious crew members drag back sliding hull doors and dip their heads out to see, then dip inside again, locking those doors fast.

We're on our own.

By the time we reach the bow, we're headed back down the riverway through Bloodtown, passing its rows of Chinese lanterns. Another glance confirms the yachts have bottlenecked into single file in pursuit. All twenty of them.

"Well, this is great," I quip.

The *Thing* hums as it pushes up to fifteen knots, sending waves splashing over the stone stairs and porches of the houses of Bloodtown, its gleaming hull barely fitting through that haunted canal. Then we're slowing down as we enter the winding section of river gorge again. Next will be the sea.

"How are we going to lose them?" I hold myself, shivering and teeth chattering, and turn to Redfearn. "What happens once we get out to open sea?"

There's a grim set to Redfearn's jaw—he doesn't know. But when we round a bend and see the great arch of the paifang ahead, his face slackens. He's come to a decision.

He pushes the yacht controller into my hands. "Back in a sec."

My jaw hangs. "What? I can't—"

"You'll do great," he says, moving past me. "Just—don't crash."

I look out beyond the bow, gobsmacked, at a total loss. This is not what I do. This is not my area of expertise. I try not to move the joystick at all, only giving it tiny taps to keep the *Thing* headed straight under the paifang. What in God's name is Redfearn—

And then the captain is beside me again, the monstrous black bulk of a rocket launcher in his arms.

My jaw hangs again. "Where the hell did *that* come from?"

Redfearn inspects the launcher, double-checks it's loaded. "Picked it up before we left Hibernacula. Saw Arie use one once. Thought it might come in handy." He shoulders the launcher and squints through its telescopic sight. "Keep her steady."

There's a *thump* and I catch the gleam of a shell arcing through the air. It explodes in a bright burst of flame into the paifang, right where its gable superstructure joins its redwood of a righthand post. Wood splinters. Chipped decorations go flying. A giant crack snakes through the paifang.

Satisfied, he turns to me. "Ready?"

"For what?"

"When I say so, use those bottom knobs for the stern thrusters to increase our speed." He glances behind at the yachts pursuing us, back at the paifang, as if gauging something. Then he lifts the rocket launcher again, closes one eye. "Now."

I ramp up the speed, kicking the *Thing* up to fifteen knots, and Redfearn fires.

The second warhead does it. It blasts apart the struts joining the gable to the post, and in a great grinding and splintering of wood, the paifang cracks clean through and begins to cave in on itself, all those shingled roofs and ornate carvings falling inward toward the righthand side.

Its shadow falls on us, and then bits of painted wood are bouncing off the deck, that slow-moving behemoth looking like it's going to bury us.

"Redfearn?" I breathe.

Then we've shot under it, its bulk inches from clipping our stern. It crashes into the estuary with a bone-rattling impact, sending a surging wave of water erupting into the night. The *Thing* dips and plunges, riding the ensuing swells, and then Redfearn and I are standing on the gangway and looking back. The aftermath is a blur of spent fury and motion, a haze of mist descending in glittering veils. We hold our breath. Then the mist dissipates into the air to reveal the gargantuan wreckage of the paifang has blocked the river mouth, trapping our pursuers in the gorge beyond.

We're safe.

I whirl to Redfearn, chest heaving, ecstatic with elation, ready to throw my arms around him—

But he stands there like a dead thing, his gaze cast far back to that river. That town. That Bloodhouse with the blood son of the Steward impaled on its roof.

THIRTY-TWO
CAPTAIN REDFEARN

The knock on the door jolts me awake.

My arm swings out, hitting something, and knocks it off the bed in a hollow clink of glass. I rub at my eyes, roll over to see the collection of empty whiskey bottles on the floor by the bed.

Oh. Right.

I roll onto my back, wincing, and press a hand to my brow as if that will put a stop to my head-splitting hangover. Or the shame.

Once it was clear we were safe, I'd gone straight to the saloon bar, grabbed an armful of my liquor of choice and locked myself in my quarters. It was an almost unbearable relief to give in after all these years. A sweet rush of freedom, the complete obliteration of all thought.

But now, it's all catching up to me again in a mortifying wave of humiliation.

Mrs. Colding raps again on the door, making me flinch. My voice, when it comes, is pitifully ragged. "Please go away."

"I'm not leaving until you let me in."

When I don't answer, the doorknob turns.

Mrs. Colding stands in the doorway a long time, taking in my state, all the bottles heaped around me. The depth of sadness, the empathy on her face—the pity—is too much to bear.

I turn my face away, my chin trembling.

The door clicks, and then I feel Mrs. Colding's weight on the bed. Right now, I know, she'd be folding her hands in her lap.

"You can't blame yourself," she begins.

"Try me."

"He was—he was a vampire—"

I roll over to give her a look. "Aye. And so's Adrian."

Mrs. Colding looks down into her lap.

"He was nothing like Pongshu," I say, "and we both know it."

"I know," Mrs. Colding concedes. "He was—I know why you felt for him. But it was his choice to do what he did. No one else's. That's not on you."

"If I hadn't have hesitated—if I'd done something, maybe he wouldn't have—"

"Stop," she sighs, shaking her head. "Don't do that to yourself." She sweeps her eyes across the bottles, over to me, a sorrowful warning in her voice. "I can't watch you do this to yourself, Redfearn. I can't watch you become this again. I know you're more than this."

Shame scorches my throat. My eyes well up. "I know," I whisper. "I'm done. It's over. I promise."

"It better be."

"I just—I feel cursed," I confess in a wavery voice, a sob threatening to come out. "Everything I touch—everyone around me seems to die or disappear—"

"Hey," Mrs. Colding says and scooches closer on the bed, grabs my face and rests her brow on mine. "You're not cursed. It's not you. Do you hear me?" She locks eyes with me. "It's not you."

I stare back into the perfect brown endlessness of her eyes, desperate for answers. "How do I change this?"

She looks down, places her hand on my heart. "I know what's in you. It's why I love you. Just trust in that. Believe in what we have."

I suck in a rattling breath, hold her hand to my heart. I muster everything in me and give her a smile. "Thank you." After this heaviness has lifted the slightest bit, I go on. "What of Penelope? Our last chance of bargaining for her is gone. How can we plan to save her if we don't even know anything about this base she's on?"

She drops her eyes, scratches gently at my chest with a finger. "I don't know." She lifts her gaze to me again. "What are you going to do?"

That I don't know. I look off to the morning light peeking through the blinds, shining on a half-empty whiskey bottle on the nightstand. I feel that tug of oblivion again and push it away with vicious force.

Then my eyes drop to my phone by the whiskey bottle, and the solution comes to me.

"I'm going to make a call."

The phone rings and rings. I haven't used this number yet. I was given it before I parted ways with Arie in Transmarinia, in case of emergencies, and a part of me doubts I'll get through.

But then, in a faint spit of static, I hear it: "Hello, old friend."

It is, unmistakably, the smooth and haunted voice of my old boss, Adrian Voper.

I find myself straightening my back. "Sir."

"Please." I can hear, even through the crackling hiss on the phone, the gentle smile in his voice. "After everything we've been through, you don't need to call me that anymore."

I nod, taking that in, a sudden pressure behind my eyes. "Thank you . . . Adrian. I didn't want to bother you, it really is a last resort—"

"Stop. I'm glad you called."

I can't help it—I have to ask. "Where are you?"

There's a silence on the line, broken only by the occasional pop of static. "It's probably best I not tell you. But Arie is . . . where she said she would be. And I'm following behind, trying to keep her as safe as I can."

"Sonofabitch, she actually did it," I marvel. "She found him."

"Yes."

"How's she doing?"

Another silence. I can hear the hard edge of worry in his voice. "I don't know."

I chew on that. "And you can't do anything. It's driving you crazy, isn't it?"

Adrian lets out a hollow, mirthless laugh. "Yes. Yes, it is."

"I don't know how I'd deal with that, either." I pause. "But it's almost done?"

Adrian doesn't seem to know how to answer this. I can hear that worry creeping back into his voice. "We're very close. Not long now." Then he pulls himself out of his thoughts. "And you? Any luck?"

Everything that's happened in the last few days comes roaring back, and my stomach clenches. I glance at the door through which Mrs. Colding left only minutes before, and my heart aches at the memory of her face as she took in the liquor bottles on the floor.

I clamp my jaw, willing my breathing steady.

"Yes," I say when I can trust my voice again. "I got my hands on the coordinates to my daughter's location, and I'm almost there now. But she's . . ." I swallow hard, a sudden lump in my throat. "One of them took her, Adrian. And I . . . I messed up the only plan I could think of to get her back."

I know him well enough to hear it in his voice. Becoming somber, dialing in to how serious this is. That I'm not exactly doing great right now.

"Tell me," he says simply.

I make the recounting as straightforward as I can. Penelope's trail ending at the Commodore's base. Me commandeering the *Thing* to get to her. The Steward's letter. *The Palace of the Fang*. When I get to the part of what I did to Pongshu, my throat gets tight. And when I get to the Bloodhouse and Jiangshi's flight through the window, it closes up on me. I don't have the heart to confess to him that I fell off the horse and started drinking again. I shake my head, eyebrows knitting together. "I don't know what to do. I'm going to get there without any of the passengers they're expecting, and I don't even know where she'll be in this godforsaken place. Let alone know how to steal her away without anyone noticing." I sit there with my chest tight and wave a hand, letting out a harsh, bitter sound that's not quite a laugh. "Any ideas?"

There's a juddering hum on his end of the line, as if that submarine yacht he's on is submerging, going dark. Or making evasive maneuvers.

I try not to think about it.

Then, at last, "Let me think on it." But he does not go. He lets out a snort, sounding impressed. "Of course Mrs. Colding insisted on going with you. I wouldn't expect anything less." His voice changes, becomes tentative. "And how's *she* doing?"

My chest grows tighter, that ache more tender. My mouth crooks in a smile. "We've gotten really close." My eyes sting, and I look up at the ceiling, determined to not let any tears fall. "But I don't know. I don't know if I'm any good for her."

Adrian doesn't rush into any response. He gives me space, knowing I need it.

I don't know when he got so goddamn emotionally intelligent.

At last, I harrumph deep in my throat. "When did you know Arie was the one?" I ask, wiping brusquely at my eyes.

Adrian considers this. "I think I knew as soon as I saw her picture from her stewardess interview. I just couldn't admit it to myself."

I let out a harsh bark of laughter, nod and drop my head.

"Honestly," he goes on, "sometimes I don't know what she sees in me. I don't know how I got so lucky."

I clutch the phone hard and nod, glancing at the door again. "Yeah," I say, and add silently, to myself, *I understand that feeling perfectly*.

CAPTAIN'S LOG

Mainland Coast to the Commodore's Base, December 11th.

Ship: *Thing.*

Speed: 25 knots.

Distance: 20 mi.

Weather: Clear, calm day.

Notes: Will reach coordinates for Volok's base within the hour.

THIRTY-THREE
MRS. COLDING

When I feel the *Thing* slow to a cautious crawl, I know we're approaching Volok's base.

My skin buzzes.

When we'd lifted anchor and resumed our course, Redfearn had appointed the first mate to take the helm and disappeared inside his quarters again. So I'm expecting to find him at the helm now that our speed has changed.

But he's not there.

"Where's the captain?" I ask the first mate, a sour-lipped Chinese man with a severe undercut who's not even watching the nav console; he's scrolling on his phone. "Who's piloting?"

The mate juts his chin, not bothering to take his eyes off his phone.

That's when I see the figure at the bow.

He's the only person out on deck. There's no sign of the crew, as if even they don't want to see the base during our stop here.

But there's no base to be seen.

As I approach Redfearn at the bow, I scan the horizon. Nothing but still water for as far as the eye can see. I don't know what I'd been expecting. Maybe the ruin of some creepy fortress clinging to a spur of rock, with a boathouse entered by a yawning seagate portcullis. An illustration out of an old shilling shocker.

But there's nothing out here. Not even a heap of rubble on a reef. Only empty ocean.

Only Redfearn.

He has the yacht controller in one hand, his chart plotter in the other, a string of coordinates punched into it: the location of Volok's base. He squints at it, looks out at the ocean again, and I almost believe he hasn't noticed me. He's shaved, put on fresh dress whites with their captain's epaulettes, and there's a calmness to him again, a cold determination about him, as if some decision has been made.

I don't know if I like it.

Not sensing an opening, I decide to stick to practical matters. "Where is it?" I ask.

His lips thin. "I don't know." He glances down at the plotter again, at the ocean around us. "We should be right on top of it."

I shake my head. "Maybe it's mobile? Like one of those offshore seasteads?"

"Maybe." He shrugs, a hollow, uncaring slumping of his shoulders. "Or maybe the crew have known who I am all along, and it's a trap set by the Nosferyachtu Club."

This fatalistic acceptance doesn't make me scared, like I expect.

It makes me angry.

"What's wrong with you?" I snap, crossing my arms. "Why won't you talk to me? You're about to leave and find your daughter, and I don't even know what your plan is. Do you *have* one?"

He swallows and stares straight ahead, avoiding my gaze. "I'll figure it out."

But somehow, I think he does have one.

One he won't tell me.

"I have contacts all around the world, you know," I remind him. "I could call one of them and get us help—"

He dismisses this. "We don't even know anything about this base. It's probably impregnable." He waves at the open ocean. "How can we plan to sneak into it if we can't find it or even know what it looks like?"

I sound sulkier than I'd like. "So you're going alone, then. Without me."

"Not after the Bloodhouse. That was a mistake."

"Maybe," I snip, going cold at the memory of all those fangs despite a rising indignation. "And maybe you wouldn't have gotten out of there without me."

He looks at me now, truly shocked I don't get it. "I will never put you in that kind of danger again."

I roll my eyes and look off into the biting wind, arms still crossed and getting crosser. I shake my head. "You're infuriating, Captain Redfearn." But try as I might against it, my heart melts, and I change tactics, laying a hand on his arm. "I wish you would tell me. I wish you'd let me in. I don't want this to be our last interaction before you go."

He studies me, debating it. I can see it in his eyes. The desire—the temptation—to give in and tell me. To share what's going on inside him.

He opens his mouth—

And the chart plotter beeps, jerking us back to reality. We stare at it.

It reads **21°44'06.2"N 113°31'29.7"E**.

We're here.

That anger swells up in me again, an anger hiding a prickling unease, a sense of being poked fun at. "This is stupid," I huff, waving an irritable hand at the emptiness before us. "Why did it bring us here—"

That's when we hear a low clank and hum beneath our feet, and the sea begins to foam.

As we watch, what looks like twin black horns rise out of the sea. But they're not horns. They rise higher and higher out of the churning water, and I see that they're in fact spires. Gleaming, metallic-looking. They're followed by walls, dripping battlements, all clad in black glass and steel like some kind of gothic skyscraper, a steep black pyramid split down the middle to form two towers. It all rises up, and up, blocking out the sun and casting us in shadow, pushed upward by what has to be pylons founded deep in the seabed below. Eighty, a hundred feet tall, the water sheeting down its polished plating, revealing—in its monstrous birth—a slick, modern update to those fantastical fortresses that housed horrors back in the dark days ruled by superstition. And I realize, with a dull beat of dread in my chest: It's not a base that the Commodore has. No. This is not Volok's base.

It's his castle.

Almost without thinking, Captain Redfearn and I find each other's hand and grip tight.

With a deep rumble the castle halts its ascent, the sea washing and roiling still about it, making the bow of the *Thing* dip and bob in its wake. Redfearn and I grip the railing to keep our footing. We hold our breath. Our ears ring with the plaintive cawing of gulls wheeling away from this rude new presence in the middle of nowhere. And then, with a hydraulic whine, a door unseals itself from the black mirror of the monolith, lowers like a drawbridge until its end is almost kissing the skin of the sea. Waiting.

An invitation has been extended.

Redfearn's throat bobs, and he lifts a crew radio to his lips. "Get the tender ready."

My stomach bottoms out. "No, wait—"

But Redfearn is already striding for the stern. I cast a look of dismay over my shoulder and follow him. "You can't be serious," I scold him, trying for some measure of calm. "Look at that thing. That's not a place you go into and come out of again. You can't—"

But he's already at the swim deck, ready to step into the tender and go on without me, leave me behind. It's all so horrifyingly familiar. But this time, he's not like he was. This time, his face is closed off, a stranger's. Some unknown resolve there.

I can't bear it.

"Redfearn. *Wait.*"

He stops at that, turns. I draw myself up, choosing my words carefully. "I don't want you going in there when you're like this."

His storm-gray eyes clear, and for a moment I see that vulnerability in him. Then he looks me full in the face, heedless of the deckhands watching, and says, "You'll see me again. I promise."

He hops into the tender, waits for the deckhands to throw the bow and stern lines inside the boat, and revs off, aiming for that castle looming impossibly out of the sea.

You'll see me again. I promise.

Why did that sound like a goodbye?

The sobs rise up, wanting out, and I can't force them down again. With a wrenching cry I stifle with the back of my hand, I turn away.

Just as with *The Palace of the Fang*, I can't watch. I can't watch him leave me. Not when I don't know if he'll come back.

I pace on the swim deck, my hands at my temples. I can feel it coming over me, that familiar twitching in my fingers, that need to clean, and hate myself for it. I wring them at my sides as if to rid them of it, then hold my stomach, as if I can keep that compulsion in check, keep in the unsteady, hiccupping breaths, the hyperventilating. But that's as futile as it always is, and the tears are pushing themselves up and out in a scalding sting of salt as I hear the drone of Redfearn's tender approach that gleaming horror. I can't refuse it—I bolt away, past the bewildered deckhands, back inside the *Thing.* I know where to go. I know what I need. I fly back to my suite, the breath hitching in my chest, the panic skirling up inside me like wind in a flue, desperate for release. But I've already detailed the suite spotless. I snarl out a sob of frustration and grab a vase, smash it to the floor. I stare at the mess in a rictus of horror and ecstasy and sink with a sob of relief to my knees, hardly able to see through the blinding tears, the blinding gratitude, and begin to scrape up the fragments with my bare hands. Here. I can fix this. This I can control. I can make this safe. He will be safe. He will be. Safe.

THIRTY-FOUR
CAPTAIN REDFERN

As I look back at Mrs. Colding sweeping away into the *Thing*, her face fierce and blotchy with tears, I know I have to push her out of my mind. If I dwell on that, let thoughts of Mrs. Colding overtake me, it will be over. I'll never go through with this. And so I turn my back on that yacht and what it contains, words running like a chant through my head:

I'm here. At last, I'm here. I've found it. I've found where you are.

I'm coming, Pen.

And I face that baroque monolith that holds my baby girl prisoner.

Castle Volok is built from darkness. There is a small iron dock cleat riveted to the end of the drawbridge, and I hop out onto cantilevered black steel with the tender's bow line in my hand and loop it tight around the horns of the cleat, make sure the boat's fenders are hung correctly. Then I take in the castle gate. It's a maw of nothing, a tunnel of black rock as polished as obsidian. The rock that can be seen is rippled, as if worn smooth by an ancient lava flow. As if the castle itself were carved out of the hollow heart of a volcano, blasted into glittering black glass.

And there is no light within. The tunnel quickly fades to darkness, and I wonder if there is any light at all in that place. If it's more than just a tomb risen from the deep.

But I'm wrong. As I watch, light begins to waken inside the tunnel entrance, an uncanny green veining, shimmering and eerie—light activated by the outside. By the sun.

The tunnel is seamed with phosphorescence.

I lean over into the tender again, rifle through a compartment in the helm and find it. A flashlight.

Gripping it hard in my hand, I approach the gate and click on the light, a blast of white brilliance almost too blinding to bear, and run the beam over the tunnel's surfaces as if it were a paintbrush. Then I click it off and wait, listening to the lapping waves, the cries of gulls, my heart pounding in my chest.

Slowly, very slowly, the tunnel comes alive, crawling with strange traceries of green phosphor, lighting my way into the castle.

Glancing back one last time at the *Thing*, I stride into Castle Volok.

The first thing that hits me is the cold; it takes the breath away. Then the quiet. The hush of the waves lapping against the castle soon fades, replaced by the sound of my footsteps echoing on the polished steel plating of the floor, the moaning of the wind in that tunnel. I expect some footman to greet me, or a rush of fangs out of the darkness. But nothing comes.

Here and there, I pass negative space in the tunnels, other passageways branching off the main one. Once, I see a faint play of light dancing on a wall and think, *So there's a marina somewhere in this castle.*

Once, I hear a voice cry out, sharp and female, and the gooseflesh puckers along my arms.

But my gut tells me I need to keep going straight ahead. That if I do, I'll find Penelope.

I can't lose my way now.

I have to click the flashlight on and off several times as I go, to keep activating the phosphor and lighting my way. Once I look back and see that the tunnel has gone dark behind me, the phosphorescence fading away to a dim glow, then nothing. I swallow.

I am a moving point of light in a limitless dark.

The fourth time I click the flashlight on to illuminate the tunnel, the beam doesn't stop close to me. It blasts on and on, unchecked, until it hits a ceiling some fifty feet above me. I've reached some kind of enormous room.

My flesh crawls. I trace the beam over the space, getting glimpses of archways, stone buttresses, the beautiful face of a carved woman with her hair frozen in waves of black marble.

Then I click the flashlight off and wait.

Little by little, the seams of phosphorescence come alive. They snake across a high vaulted ceiling, down and around rows of pillars holding up all that rock, over archways and up plinths and the statues of women atop them, a silent company with eyes dead and staring, caught. One of them, I note with a dull thrum of disgust, is unmistakably Evangeline Voper.

His brides. All these are the likenesses of Volok's brides.

And this is his hall. The hall of the Commodore.

It slowly reveals its dark splendor to me in the uncanny glow of brightening phosphor. Long and immense, brutally architectured. And I finally see, at the far end, a dais of many steps. On the top of those steps stands a spiky black throne awaiting the return of its master. At the bottom and off to the side, a bleak stone chair, small and plain.

There is a man sitting in that chair.

I jolt. My pulse thuds in my ears. My breath goes dead in my chest. I turn cold all over.

The Steward lifts his head and smiles at me. "Captain Malter, I trust."

I unstick my tongue from the roof of my mouth. "Yes, sir."

The Steward rises. He is thin, tall, wrapped only in a shimmering Oriental robe, the only color besides the phosphor in that hall. But he is not Asian. He is a white man. Very, very white. His skin as pale as a deep-sea slug. I can see the dull gleam of his flat chest above the folds of the robe, his sharp-clawed hands as they cinch the sash tight around his waist. His face is still in shadow.

Soft black slippers hush across the polished floor toward me. His long, pale hands are clasped behind him. His words are soft, carefully phrased, as if he hasn't always spoken this way, as if it is a learned thing. An act he is putting on.

"I have been wondering what sort of man you'd be." He takes in my dress whites, my build, my face with its cuts and bruises from the past few days, and I feel as if my very soul is being dissected on a coroner's slab. "Not what I was expecting, given the stories that are told about you."

My skin creeps.

"Your predilections are not far from mine, I hear. I would ask if you and Pongshu enjoyed yourselves during the crossing . . ." He makes a show of looking around me. "But I cannot help but notice that my blood son is not with you. Nor the other cargo."

My mouth is completely dry now; it hurts to swallow. "There were . . . complications."

The Steward slows, cocks his head: *Go on*.

"You know your son. He got carried away, went into a feeding frenzy and sampled all the passengers before we got here. They . . . didn't make it." I shrug. "Pongshu knew you'd be angry and fled. I don't know where he is."

The Steward stares at the floor as he listens to this explanation, one pale hand rising to tap a talon against his lips. "That does sound like Pongshu." His thin shoulders shrug in his robe. "Oh well. He will find his way back to me eventually."

The carelessness, the flippancy—it brings on a swift pulse of anger.

You are no father, I spit at him silently.

"But." The Steward stops with his back to me, as if hearing this, and lifts a talon. "You coming to me empty-handed does beg the question . . ."

My gut clenches.

He turns to me, and in the shadows of that face I see his eyes glow, the tips of his fangs gleam. "Why bother?"

I grope for words, my mind racing. "I felt it only right that I—"

"Why bother coming at all when you had failed your task?" he presses on in a treacherous whisper. "Hmm, Captain Malter?" He steps closer, the shadows receding, showing me more teeth and a hooked nose, eyes still shaded under the ledge of his porcelain brow. "Or should I say . . . *Captain Redfearn?*"

The world stills.

My stomach turns over. Sweat pushes out of me. I fight to keep my face unreadable under the Steward's probing gaze.

At last, those womanly lips lift up, exposing more fang. "You think you could make such a fuss at *The Palace of the Fang* without me hearing about it? Or in Bloodtown, for that matter?" The Steward tuts, shaking his head in disappointment. "You insult me, Captain."

I can only stare. The blood has drained from my brain; it is utterly useless, stricken blank with panic. With a flurry of agitated thoughts.

He knows. It's all changed now. There's only one thing left to do. One thing left to say.

But the Steward does not need me to say anything. He prefers to continue speaking himself.

"No. I know why you bothered," he intones. "Because you had cargo of your own you wished to pick up."

My heart stops.

"When I learned of your determination to find me, it made me wonder . . ." The Steward spreads his arms, taking in the soaring hall. "Why? And there seemed only one possible answer: The reason was already here." He taps the side of his nose, gives me a sly wink. "From there, it didn't take long to find out which one it was."

And he steps aside . . .

Revealing, behind him, the chair he vacated at the foot of the dais is no longer empty. A sleeping woman is slumped sideways across it now, one bare leg drooping to the floor, her head and one arm flung back over an armrest, as if she had swooned there in a fit of love or terror.

It's Penelope.

The hall quivers. "No," I breathe, all composure forgotten. "Pen? Pen!"

The cold floor blurs under my feet, my footfalls echoing in that vast throne room. I glimpse a tiny smirk on the Steward's face as I brush past him, and then I'm brushing my daughter's matted blonde hair back from her brow, taking her face in my hands. She is deathly pale. "Pen?" I whisper, and the word chokes in my throat. "It's me, baby. It's Daddy. I came for you. Everything's going to be all right now."

I can barely see; everything is blurring, becoming hot. I place my brow to hers, my body torn between great, tearing sobs and laughs of blinding relief. "I'm here, baby," I choke. "Daddy's here. Daddy's going to get you out of this place." I pull back to look at her. She still has those stubborn eyebrows she got from me, the pouty, willful twist of the lips she got from her mother. And she is in a flimsy white nightdress and nothing else. There's a bruise on her throat, bracketed by two pairs of holes. They're wounds. Puncture wounds.

Bite marks.

There's more of them. They continue in a dark trail down her chest, onto the swell of her breasts, her shoulders, her arms, her legs. Even, I see, as I twitch her dress into a more modest position, on the tender flesh of her inner thighs.

My hand freezes, a muscle jerking under my eye.

"What did you do to her?" I hoarse when I can speak again.

The Steward's voice dances back to me: light, airy, scornful. "Do not worry, Captain. She's merely drugged. It helps keep her more ... compliant." Soft, soft laughter. "She has fire, like you. Perhaps that is why she is my favorite."

Everything goes red.

In one smooth motion I've stood, pulling out Lelouch's Glock that's been jammed into the back of my khaki shorts. "You sick fuck—"

"Ah-ah." The Steward ticks a finger, stopping me. "I wouldn't."

I scan the hall. Pale-faced, black-clothed shadows have appeared all around it, gliding out from under archways, between pillars. Perhaps twenty of them. Standing in sinister silence and warning like a host of assassinous manservants.

The Steward purses his lips in triumphant scorn. "Neither of you would get out of here alive."

No, I think, the fear trebling in me. *But then, a part of me knew I wouldn't. Or rather, I knew a part of me wouldn't.*

And the fear, suddenly, is gone. It's replaced by a vast unfurling calm, of something like acceptance.

Yes. Yes. This was always going to happen.

I shut my eyes.

And then: "Is that what you want?"

My eyes snap open. I slowly swivel my head toward the Steward, lower the gun. "I have a different idea."

"Oh?" The Steward bares his fangs in a curious, considering smile. "What is it, Captain Redfearn? What are you willing to do to get your daughter back?"

And we stand there looking at each other, the eerie phosphorescence seaming the hall dying around us like the failing electrical impulse in a heart, fading away until I'm speaking my answer into blackness as dark as the pit.

"I have a proposition for you."

"I have a proposition for you."

CAPTAIN'S LOG

The Commodore's Base, December 12th.
Ship: *Thing.*
Speed: At anchor.
Weather: Calm dusk.
Notes: I love you, Penelope. I love you more than I can bear. I will do anything for you. Anything.

THIRTY-FIVE

MRS. COLDING

It's the longest hour of my life before I see them return.

I can't believe it. I stand on the aft main deck in a daze as I watch Captain Redfearn bear his daughter in his arms up the steps toward me. She is sleeping, her head hanging back in the lemony sunlight of late day, her bare legs and the skirt of a white nightdress trailing from his arms. Her perfect, dirt-smudged face is childish and headstrong with its proud, sculpted lips and stern nostrils, its shock of dark eyebrows. Her mother must be a beautiful woman.

But I don't understand. I don't know how this came to be. All I know is I am in a tizzy of joy.

"What happened?" I ask, touching Redfearn's arm, my heart thumping in my chest. "How did you do it?"

He stops to look at me. He seems infinitely tired, his face drawn, the wrinkles deep around his eyes. But there is a lightness there. An old burden lifted.

He stares off at the castle. It is sinking again into the waves, all that gleaming black steel and glass descending again into the watery darkness below in a burbling of foam, as if it has served its purpose. "The Steward is a father, too," he says, almost too soft to hear. "I appealed to that side of him." Then he turns to me, and happiness reaches his eyes now. He smiles. "Let's get out of here."

We've docked in the Port of Macau by nightfall. We disembark under the lights of the city's glitzy high-rises with Redfearn carrying his daughter, me pulling our two roller bags down the maze of gangways behind me. I look back and the crew of the *Thing* are watching us go, looking somewhat lost without us, waiting for their next captain and chief stew to take command and continue their miserable voyages to that sunless castle in the South China Sea. A cursed crew of an accursed ship.

I can't believe it's over. A small, guilty part of me had thought this would all end in tragedy and death. Me losing Redfearn. Perhaps myself.

But miracles can happen. He is here with me, straight-backed and capable as he waits for me to get the door of the dockside hotel for us. Then we are inside and the *Thing* is lost to view. We have left that behind. We have left danger and tragedy behind us.

We are moving forward now.

We book two rooms. One for Penelope, one for Redfearn and myself. I watch Redfearn lay her down on the bed and pull the covers to her chin, kiss her brow and whisper in her ear. I can barely hear the words.

"My little sun," he says. "My little sun."

I don't know why, but it makes my chin quiver.

"You think she'll be okay in here?" I ask when I'm able to.

"She's been drugged," he growls, a hint of anger there as he writes a brief note and sticks it on the nightstand for her to see when she wakes. "She'll be asleep for a while yet."

In the room next door, the note reads. *218. I love you. Your father.*

"We need to rest, too," he says as he walks back to me, and takes my hand. His eyes are red. "Then we'll be there when she wakes."

I nod, and he eases the door shut behind him as quietly as he can, leads me to our room.

We're too exhausted to do anything but crawl into bed. He lies on his back with a groan, the bounce of his weight knocking his bag onto the floor, landing it on its side. I'm about to kneel and stand it on its wheels when he grabs my wrist. "It's okay. Leave it."

"Just doesn't look right," I mutter, my hands twitching, and start to bend over.

But he—gently, firmly—holds my wrist in place. "Hey," he says, and waits for me to look at him. "Perfection doesn't exist. You can let it go."

I open my mouth, cheeks burning, my conviction wavering. Then I kick his bag so it lands flat on its back. At least it's no longer hideously positioned on its side.

"There," I announce. "All better."

He shakes his head as I crawl into bed, the tiniest of smirks tucked into one corner of his mouth. "You are something else."

"Let's not pretend you don't find it adorable, shall we?" I sniff and curl up against him, my head on his shoulder, my hand on his chest.

"Let's not," he agrees. "But still. One day I'll help you let go of it, so you can be that free spirit I know is hiding under that bun of yours."

My heart knocks strangely, humbled and embarrassed, yet hushed with a gratitude and recognition I'm not ready to face. I trace the buttons of his white yachtie polo with a finger to distract myself. "I still don't know how you did it," I marvel at last, in a whisper.

After a beat, he grunts. "I can be persuasive when I want to be."

I smile. "This I know." I prop my temple on my fist and look at him, taking in those rugged features I know so well. That strong jaw with its glittery silver of stubble. The dashing salt-and-pepper sweep of his hair. His gray eyes the color of sea mist. "So what now?"

He smiles at my flirtatiousness, something wistful and pained in that dimpling of his cheeks, and brushes the backs of his knuckles along the curve of my jaw. "You ready to leave the yachting world behind for good?"

My lips pert. "Are you trying to scare me?"

He snorts. "Nothing scares you."

I swallow the sudden lump in my throat, hold his hand against my cheek. "The idea of losing you does." The skin around his eyes slackens, and I blink back a sting of tears. "I thought I did lose you, after Pongshu. And then today . . . today I thought . . ."

To my mortification, my voice gets all wavery and cracked, and Redfearn shushes me, taking my face in both his hands. "Hey," he says, soft and stern, his eyes locking with mine. "You will always have my love. Always. You understand?"

I nod, eyes brimming with tears. They plume and bead my lashes, blurring everything away.

When I can see again, he's taking something out of his pocket. A small jewelry box. I push myself up, my heart knocking in my chest. He meets my eyes and smiles. "I've been wanting to give you this for a while now." He opens the lid, lifts out what's inside. It's a necklace. Silver, with a fine, elegant chain, a pendant hanging from it: a crescent moon. "You've always been there to light my world when everything was dark. Have always shown me the way. My sailor moon."

He clasps it around my neck, and I hold the pendant in my palm, watch the light catch in that silver half-moon.

"Who needs a navigator when I have you?"

My eyes are blurring up again, a lump forming in my throat. "Redfearn," I croak.

His brows come down. "Do you—do you like it?"

I don't say anything. Because I'm kissing him, hard and fierce, making a low, mewling noise into his mouth. That sound of need makes him draw me to him, crushing me to the delicious warmth of his body, and then I'm rolling on top of him with my yachtie skirt riding up my thighs, that precious necklace dangling over him, and I straighten and lift my hands up to undo my hair, let it down from its bun. A ceremony. *Yes*, I'm saying as I let all that silky darkness tumble about my shoulders and he gazes up at me with lips parted. *I'm willing to show you the real me. The person who is not a yachtie. The person whose identity I haven't even figured out yet.*

I'll take all that icy armor off and show her to you, naked and exposed, with nowhere to hide.

He knows it, too. He knows what this means. A great tenderness gentles his face and he sits up to kiss me, one hand sweeping behind my neck to bury itself in my hair, wrap me close. A great heaviness gathers between my thighs. My nipples perk. Then I'm pulling at his belt and taking him out, and I hear him groan as I tug my panties to the side and lower myself onto him.

He shudders, mouth open, lost in the feeling, and I smooth my hands over his face, his broad brow, his stubbled cheeks, and our eyes catch. What I see there is so raw, so real and filled with wonder and dazzling heartache, it makes me have to bite the inside of my lip to keep from sobbing. And through all this, I begin to ride him. Slowly at first, then with more and more urgency. He does not look away, does not blink, and I feel my cheeks flare with heat. His hands follow the curve of my back, stopping just above my ass to tuck me against him, hold me close. The steamy intimacy of his hard stomach against mine, his groin against mine, is almost too much to bear. Then his hands are picking at my shirt, unbuttoning it to reveal that pendant dangling in my cleavage, parts it fully to reveal my breasts. I watch him, open-mouthed. He traces a finger down my sternum, over the pendant, lets it stray so he can cup a breast in his hand. Then his warm mouth is skimming over my collarbone, his tongue and teeth finding my pulse at the base of my throat, dipping to suck my nipple long and hard.

I shut my eyes. I feel dizzy. I feel obliterated in his love.

The pleasure spreads, tingling and crackling, his touch sending goose bumps rippling down my spine, and then my nails are scoring his shoulders and back, leaving behind bright red streaks.

"Baby," I whisper, and my use of this word, for the first time, sends a growl emanating out of his chest.

It tips me over the edge.

I gasp and furiously grind on him, the pleasure blazing deep into my center, and I let out the sounds now I never could with any other man, the sounds that before would have made me feel so vulnerable I'd want to hide my face in my hands.

He loves it. He growls deep in his chest, his hand winding tight in my hair, pulling my head back. Then his breath is shallow and fast against my bared throat, turning into helpless curses, and when he comes I bend down to take his moans into my mouth.

It's a heart-melting kiss, long and indulgent, the kind of kiss that leaves my lips swollen and tingling, my body limp. When we part, he lays his head against my sternum, between my breasts, and shuts his eyes. A lump grows in my throat. I hold him to me with almost motherly tenderness, my hands tangled in his silvery hair, my heart suffused with love. *I love you, Redfearn,* I tell him silently. *You have me, in every way a person can have another. Everything's okay now. We can work through anything. I will always be by your side. I will always be yours.*

This is our love.

Afterward, I lie draped over him in the sheets, drowsy with content and warm safety. I'm slipping off into the welcome oblivion of sleep when I feel him gently slide out from under me, place a kiss on my brow. "Baby," I mumble.

"My sailor moon," he replies.

I start awake without knowing why. I listen for a moment, expecting I'm not sure what, but there's nothing to be heard. Somewhere far off, a horn drones. Some kind of tanker in the harbor. I rub the sleep from my eyes and roll over, reaching out across the sheets—but Redfearn isn't beside me.

I jerk upright in bed and look about, unwanted premonition narrowing my throat, thumping in my chest. The hotel room is empty, the sliding glass door leading onto the balcony open to the humid night air. The curtains loft gently in the breeze.

"Redfearn?" I call, the beginnings of a cold fear gathering in my gut.

His leatherbound captain's log is on the table. It's open, its white pages gleaming in the moonlight, as if beckoning. There's a fresh entry written there, dated tonight.

A shudder works its way down my spine.

I pick up the log and begin to read.

After a few seconds, my hands begin to tremble. The tears push into my eyes, making the words wriggle and dance on the page. My bottom lip quivers. "No," I say, shaking my head, the breaths suddenly coming in sharp, catastrophic gasps. "Oh God . . . oh God . . ." I whirl to see, and it's true: his roller bag my OCD made me kick flat is gone.

The log slips from my nerveless fingers to the floor as I drop to my knees.

"*NOOOOOOOOOOOOOO!*"

CAPTAIN'S LOG

Port of Macau, December 12th.
Ship: *Thing*.
Speed: At anchor.
Weather: Clear night.
Notes: I'm sorry to leave you both like this. You cannot know how sorry I am. But I have to go, and I know it would only be more painful while you're both awake.

I wish we could have had a chance to explore what this could have been, Mrs. Colding. I would have loved you with everything I had. But I think we both know I would've fucked it up, just like my marriage. And I don't know if I could bear breaking your heart.

And you, Pen—if you woke, and I got to be with you for the first time in years, I wouldn't have the heart to leave.

And so I have to abandon you again, like I did all those years ago.

I'm so sorry.

I hope you can find it in your hearts to forgive me. There was no other way. I would never leave that place with Penelope alive, and so I did the only thing I could do with creatures like that.

I made a bargain.

It won't be so bad. Really. I can live with it, knowing I gave you a life again, Pen. That maybe, maybe, I found a way to earn your love again.

And if not, I understand. I know I don't deserve it. It's become clear to me I don't deserve your love. Either of yours. There is something wrong with me I can't make right, and I will have to live with that. But maybe this is the closest I can get. This way, I get to take Penelope's place, and be the Steward's new blood slave and captain of the *Thing* for as long as she sails. And this way, I won't hurt anyone else. At least, not either of you.

I'd call that more than a fair trade.

I hope you both live long and happy lives. I hope you find a better man than I am, Mrs. Colding. And I hope you find someone who takes care of you better than I did, Pen. You both deserve that.

You're my little sun, Pen. And you're my sailor moon, Mrs. Colding. Always.

I love you.

– A.R.

THIRTY-SIX
CAPTAIN REDFEARN

Castle Volok bubbles up from the deep like a demon kingdom.

I witness its rise from the helm of the tender bobbing on the dark waves, the *Thing* at anchor behind me. I left the crew of that ship behind in Macau, as I knew I had no more need of them. All the same, I fancy I see them lining the rails. A crew of the damned watching me like forlorn spirits, like psychopomps come to bring me to death's door. To far hell-gate. My flesh crawls and I look past them to where Macau must be, the hotel where I left Penelope in her ignorant slumber, Mrs. Colding mumbling my name in her sleep. A pain pinches my heart, so deep and searing it takes my breath away, and I force myself to look again to Castle Volok, to turn my back on that life. On my loves. On love.

"I'm sorry," I whisper as the drawbridge of Castle Volok lowers, inviting me inside. "I'm sorry."

There's something I have to do.

"There's one other thing," Adrian had said on that phone call in my captain's quarters.

"What's that?"

"If this happens, if Arie actually pulls this off and kills the Commodore . . ." Adrian drew in a measured breath. "Everything will change. The last vestiges of that reign will have to be erased. Do you understand?"

I waited, not knowing what he was getting at.

"The Steward, Arnold," Adrian went on. "He's a threat. And he'll always pose a threat, as long as he survives and that place he stewards stands as a symbol of Volok's reign."

I swallowed hard in my throat, a great discomfort twisting at my insides. "What are you asking of me, Adrian?"

There was a long silence on the phone, filled with the pop and crackle of static, the black roar of distance on the line. "I would appreciate it if you could take him out, Arnold, if you have the chance. Make sure Arie is safe. Can you do that for us?"

And I had lifted my eyes at hearing this, a new resolve—a new purpose—pouring into me like molten iron into a mold, taking on its inevitable shape.

"Yeah," I'd said. "Yeah, I can do that."

This time, it does not take me long to find the hall of Castle Volok; I know my way now. I click off the flashlight and wait for that throne room to come alive in a veining of eerie green light, jam the flashlight into the waistband of my khaki shorts at my back and let my hand drift over to make sure the other thing I brought is still there, too.

Yes. It is.

Lelouch's Glock, cold and loaded.

I let my hands hang at my sides.

The hall brightens, revealing the lithe form of the Steward sitting in his lowly stone chair. He is wearing another Oriental robe, this one a resplendent purple shimmeringly patterned with coils of dragon scales rubbing against each other, here and there ravening jaws emerging from the patterns.

Long, elegant fangs bare in a self-satisfied smile. "You honored your bargain."

I snort as I approach, my footsteps echoing in the hall. "We both know you would have sent killers after me if I didn't."

The Steward's smile widens. "True." He rises from his chair, clasps his hands before him like the long, bulb-knuckled legs of spiders and inclines his head, the sharp V of his black hairline contrasting with the corpselike pallor of his skin. Waiting.

"Are you ready to show your fealty?" he croons.

I stop before him, my face giving him my answer.

"Then kneel," he sneers, lips twisting in perverted pleasure.

The floor is cold and hard on my bare knee, the hall's silence absolute. All I can see is those hideous hands with their clawlike nails, spike-toothed dragon heads arcing out of seas of scales, ready to consume me.

"Well?"

He is waiting for me to offer him my bare wrist so he can sink his fangs into it, mark me as his, submissive and forever bound to him. Damned.

That will be my moment. When he is lost in that ecstasy, drunk on the rapture of my blood, I will pull the gun from my waistband, place its barrel under his chin and watch it blow his brains out of that sleek, revolting head.

I look to my right, my left, taking in our audience. The rows of silent footmen in their black frogged jackets, fangs gleaming in the dim aura of phosphorescence.

Of course, I will never make it out alive.

But it will be worth it. I will have done what I was asked. I will have been of some purpose in this life.

Arie and Penelope will be safe.

And standing amongst those sinister footmen, there's another figure, also in black. It gleams in a tactical wetsuit, its goggles turned to panes of neon green light in the glow of phosphorescence, like the eyes of an alien. My old, violent self.

It nods, giving me permission.

Slowly, and with great ceremony, I lower my head and sweep one hand behind my back as if in a courtly bow, but really so I can lift up the hem of my yachtie polo, grip the polymer handle of that hidden Glock.

And I lift the wrist of my other hand, offering it to the Steward of Castle Volok.

The hall seems to hold its breath. My heart hammers, pumping blood into my ears, into my wrist, filling me with hot life ready to be taken.

Do it, I think.

But the Steward does not take it.

"Of course," he sniffs and sweeps away, leaving my wrist hanging, "there is the small matter of you murdering my blood sons."

My stomach hollows out. The blood drains from my brain, leaving me cold and lightheaded.

"You did kill them, didn't you?" the Steward hisses as he paces before me.

My jaw works. I clamp my molars until they pop, feeling a bewildering pressure behind my eyes. "Yes," I husk.

"Then you'll understand, as a father yourself, what that kind of grief might feel like."

I think of Penelope's angry teenage face turning away from me. I think of her cradled against my chest as I carry her up the stairs to Mrs. Colding, to what should have been a new family.

I think of leaving her behind once more.

"Yes," I husk again, my voice starting to break up now.

"Then you'll understand," the Steward whispers, bending close to speak into my ear, "that you'll have to be punished for what you did."

I stare straight ahead, my chin working, my lips pressed together to keep my face composed. To stop the sting of tears in my nostrils. The almost unbearable gratitude that will make me fall apart.

This. This is it.

I almost laugh in sheer, lunatic joy. It must be some kind of divine providence, a long-fated and ruthless justice, a balancing of the scales that will leave me cleansed and free. Free from this pain.

I deserve this. I deserve this punishment.

Maybe, this way, I can be reborn.

And slowly, very slowly, I let go of the gun in the waistband of my shorts, and that frogman specter of my old self fades away into the shadows, finally released.

"I expect nothing less from a father," I gruff, the last word a choked-back sob, and lift my chin. "You do what you have to do."

I can feel it, by my face: that sharp smile, elegant fangs gleaming white as ivory.

Then his hands on me, strikingly cold, and he is tipping my head to the side, baring my neck.

I am not afraid. I wait, hushed and trembling in a dark thrill of acceptance, like a monk ready to set himself on fire.

Then his breath on my flesh, drawing out a shivering of goose bumps. That breath drags in, a ghastly shuddering of air, like a dragon preparing to unleash a storm of flame and death.

I shut my eyes.

Then I hear that voice I never thought I'd hear again.

"That's quite enough of that, thank you."

The Steward's head snaps up in a snarl. There's a stirring in the shadows, all turning to see. All dumbfounded as a figure in a gleaming black wetsuit steps out of the darkness of the tunnel, and I think, *No. I made my choice. I let you go. I'm not that anymore.*

And Mrs. Colding steps barefoot into the light, still dripping from the sea, looking as fierce and beautiful as I've ever seen her.

"Let him go," she orders and lifts up, in her clenched fist, an explosives detonator blinking red. "Or you all can bear witness to the wrath of a chief stewardess."

THIRTY-SEVEN
MRS. COLDING

After some time, I come back to myself.

My face is in my hands, my hands on my knees as I kneel there on the floor of the hotel room in Macau. I had shut down. My survival instincts kicked in, as they do, and I switched off all emotion. Now I am drained, spent of all passion.

It comes back, though, when I rise like a sleepwalker and drift to the balcony, look down into the harbor and see the *Thing* is gone, its berth empty. The irrefutable proof of what he has done.

The cursed captain of that accursed ship, taking command of her for one last voyage.

The last voyage of Captain Redfearn.

My throat lumps up. My breathing gets high and tight in my chest, that nervous agitation taking over, making my fingers twitch. I can't do this. I can't think about this. I need to clean. Now. I need to lose myself in my old coping mechanisms. But this room—it was just cleaned for our arrival. It's spotless. Nothing to fix.

So I resort to what I did last time. I grab a vase off the table and smash it on the floor. But that's not enough. Not nearly enough this time. So I grab more. A coffee mug. A plate. A mirror.

All of it, one after the other, goes shattering on the floor in pretty explosions of glass and ceramic, turning the floor into a minefield of glittering shards.

And I tower over it all like a madwoman, chest heaving, hair wild, feeling an almost transportive euphoria at the relief of having all this to clean . . .

And I freeze, Redfearn's words echoing in my mind: *Let it go.*

The blood stops in my veins.

For I know. If I give in to this distraction now, I won't be able to stop. I'll be transfixed in this trauma, and by the time I pull myself out of it, it will be too late. My chance will have slipped away. I'll have lost Redfearn forever.

(*I'll help you let go of it.*)

(*Let it go. Let it go.*)

(*Be that free spirit.*)

(*Be free.*)

And I know, finally, what he was saying. He wasn't just talking about my OCD. It was what that OCD was masking. What it was stopping me from doing.

He was saying it's time. Time for me to stop being someone who takes orders from some spoiled yacht owner so I don't have to make any decisions for myself. Time for me to stop being a bystander in my own life and take charge.

And slowly, agonizingly, as if overcoming a seizure, I curl my hands into fists and lift my eyes, jaw clenched. A tear streaks like a falling star down my cheek.

"Thank you, Redfearn," I breathe, my voice breaking, and clutch the half-moon pendant of his necklace in my hand.

I go out on the balcony to make the call.

I pat at my hair, feeling a sense of calm again—a sense of groundedness in myself—now that it's been severely twisted back up into its bun.

I'm ready for what's next.

My contact picks up on the third ring. "Mrs. Colding!" he sing-songs in cheerful wickedness. "The coldest bitch of the seven seas. It's been a while."

A faint smile tugs at my mouth, but the joy in it is dampened, distant. "Hello, Chung." I squint into the whipping wind up here, my back firmly turned on the untouched disaster in the hotel room, and take in the blinking neon magic of Macau. It's no surprise it's called the Vegas of the East: casinos are everywhere here. Tall, sweeping, magnificent, turning the harbor waters into a blaze of light. They can't help but remind me, with a dull thud in my stomach, of Captain Redfearn. And the gamble I'm about to take myself.

I force myself to swallow. "I need to call in a favor."

"Of course. Anything for my ice queen. What your guests want this time? Coke? Girls? Dom Pérignon by seaplane?"

"Something a little different this time, actually," I admit, gazing out past the flashiness of Macau to the benighted sea beyond. "And I need it yesterday."

Curious glee creeps into Chung's voice. "What did you have in mind?"

After I hang up, I go out into the hall and pause before Penelope's door. I lift a hand, debating if I should knock, then decide against it. A few minutes later I return and slip a note under the door. "Back soon," I promise in a whisper. "I'm sorry I can't stay and tell you. But I don't have time." I hesitate a moment longer, praying her sedative won't wear off before I'm back. Before *we're* back.

I wrench loose from any feelings of guilt and march off down the hall.

A quarter of an hour later, I zip up my 3mm black wetsuit and throw the dock line to Chung's contacts, rev the engine and point the bow of the lightweight skiff out to sea, checking to make sure I'm on course for the coordinates punched into Redfearn's chart plotter. The coordinates for Castle Volok.

I'm coming, Redfearn, I tell the horizon as the bow galumphs across the waves, misting my cheeks with sea spray. *I'm coming for you. And there's nothing stopping me.*

I'm able to get there far faster than the *Thing* did. The first thing I see are those black horns glinting in the moonlight, and my heart lurches into my throat. It's above water, its drawbridge lowered. Which means he made it. He's there. He's inside.

And sure enough, the *Thing* is at anchor nearby, dreaming away in its twinkling of deck lights, no crew to be seen.

I slow the skiff to a low drone and nose toward the castle.

Its immensity is no less impressive at night. It towers before the moon, cutting into that cratered white coin with its sleek black bulk, its gleaming battlements of glass and steel. I scope those many windows, but there's no way of knowing if anyone is watching. I can only pray they're not.

When I'm only twenty feet from the base of the castle, I kill the skiff's engine and wait. Waves break against the fortress in explosions of white spume, surging up and dropping away in deep troughs, revealing glimpses of metal encrusted with barnacles and furred green with beards of algae, like flashes of exposed and rusting rebar.

That's where the castle must be mounted onto the pylons.

But there's no knowing how deep they go, how big they are. I can only hope I brought enough.

I drag a waterproof dry bag toward me and loosen its neck, pull out a pair of black swim fins and slip them on. Next, a snorkel mask and Scorkl, one of those mini compressed air tanks with a regulator and mouthpiece attached directly to the cylinder. Chung's contacts said it had enough air supply for me to breathe underwater for ten minutes. I can only hope that's enough time for what I have to do. And that no one will spot my boat before I resurface.

Then I pull out a weighted diving belt with a dozen pockets attached to it, buckle it around my waist and open one of the pockets to check they're still there.

Small adherable explosives. Bulky and blinking with acceptor lights for remote control detonation.

I test the Scorkl's purge button, check to make sure the pressure indicator is less than 50 bar. Then taking a few deep breaths, I pop the Scorkl's regulator into my mouth and sit on the gunwale of the skiff, stare up at Castle Volok.

An ethereal figure stands in the shadowy entrance, a banner of lustrous blonde hair lofting in the wind: Evangeline Voper. Her fangs gleam in the moonlight, making the scars on my neck crawl and itch, promising terrors upon terrors waiting for me within that place.

My spine tingles with a shudder, and I straighten it. I hold the half-moon on my necklace.

I love you, Redfearn, I think, a fierce promise, and fall backward into the sea.

THIRTY-EIGHT
CAPTAIN REDFEARN

"How," I stammer at Mrs. Colding standing there in the throne room of Castle Volok. "How did you—"

"Careful," Mrs. Colding tuts, lifting the detonator higher, and the shadows that had begun creeping toward her freeze. She lifts her chin, the necklace I gave her glittering on her chest, and addresses the entire hall. "There is a kiloton of explosives attached to the pylons of this shitty fucking rathole," she explains with such exquisite calm that, under different circumstances, it would send me pumping my fist into the air. "So if you want to displease me and have your world destroyed, by all means"—she waggles the detonator—"displease me."

No one moves. The throne room is completely silent, pulsing with the dying glow of phosphor.

Mrs. Colding sweeps the room with her forbidding gaze, using it to challenge everyone present, and it snags on the statue of Evangeline Voper. Her face whitens, the fang-mark scars on her neck shining silver in the light of that phosphorescence, and her nostrils thin as she forces herself to look away.

Then her gaze drops to me, and it gentles. She swallows, a flicker of anxiety in her now, as if she were addressing a wild foal. "Redfearn."

A hard lump forms in my throat.

"I know why you came here," she says, "and I understand. It's very—it's very honorable." She swallows back a sheen of tears. "But you're wrong. You *are* worthy of love."

I jerk my face away, shutting my eyes against those words.

"You are," she goes on, her voice full of so much aching sympathy I could sob. "I know you've convinced yourself you deserve this punishment, but you don't. No one deserves that. Running away won't solve anything. That's the easy way out. Staying and loving your daughter—loving me—loving *yourself*—that's what's hard. The days and nights of it. The struggling with it. But it can change. I can help you change it, if you'll just let me love you."

I have a hand over my eyes by the end of this speech. I shake my head, the words cracking in my throat. "I can't."

"You can."

I steal a glance at the Steward. "He'll never leave us be."

Mrs. Colding blinks at him, as if just noticing him for the first time, trying to place him. She probably can't even make out his features in this dim hall from where she stands. I'm just surprised he's not a smoking crater after that look.

She returns her gaze to me. "We'll figure that out." She offers a hand. "Come on."

I take in a deep, wavering breath. "I don't know. I don't know if I can come back—"

"Captain Redfearn!" she snaps, all her gentleness gone in an instant, replaced with that forbidding chief stewardess demeanor that can annihilate with a glance. "I thought I couldn't stand messes, but I swear to high heaven—so help me—if you don't get up this instant and honor my love for you, nothing would make me happier than to make the biggest bloody mess I have ever seen. So. Now that I've shown I'm starting to see the appeal of chaos and destruction . . ." Her eyes narrow. "Get up, Redfearn. On your feet. *Now.*" When I don't move, her nostrils flare, the veins jumping out in her neck as she screams at me with all the passion I've always known was in her: "*GET UP!*"

And I do. I lurch to my feet as if I've been electrocuted, shocked with a thousand volts of lightning. As if I've been brought back to life. And then I'm marching toward Mrs. Colding, my heart bursting with a feeling I can't name, my eyes brimming up. No one has ever fought for me like that. No one has ever proven their love to me like that. No one has ever risked everything to love me.

Maybe—maybe—there is something in me worth loving, after all.

I don't care that all these undead fuckers are watching. When I get to Mrs. Colding I crush her to me, crush her lips to mine, showing her with every fiber of my being that I was worth it. I was worth coming back for.

I promise I will make you happy, Mrs. Colding.

And when I pull away and look into her misty eyes, I know. She heard it. She understands.

She takes my hand in hers, and we face the Steward.

"We're leaving now," Mrs. Colding declares, lifting the blinking detonator once more, and I pull out the Glock as we begin to back away. "You'll never see us again."

The Steward does not reply. He grows smaller and smaller, an inconsequential figure beside that chair guarding the throne of the Commodore. And though he isn't moving, his footmen are. They pace us along the rows of pillars lining the hall, and when I look up, I see that the ceiling is crawling. That more shadows, more of the undead, are swarming out of nooks and crannies in the stone buttresses like rats, crawling unnaturally down phosphor-seamed rock toward us, funneling toward the tunnel leading out to the sea and escape.

Goosepimples bump up all over my body.

"I think it's time to go," I whisper, pointing my Glock at one creature, then another, the threat of its firepower barely keeping them at bay.

Mrs. Colding's eyes are locked on the statue of Evangeline, a small muscle twitching at the corner of her mouth. "I think you're right," she agrees.

When we reach the mouth of the tunnel, we bolt and run. We duck as we pass into it, just missing the swiping claws of the undead boiling down the walls. Mrs. Colding cries out, a sound of fury and terror, and when I take out the flashlight and click it on, sweeping the beam behind us, a deluge of vampires is closing on our heels, crawling on the walls and ceiling, squinting and snarling in the sudden glare.

"Oh God," Mrs. Colding pants.

"Keep going," I bark, and squeeze off a few rounds behind us.

The shots are deafening in that tunnel. They light up the blackness for the briefest of moments, showing a couple of bodies dropping from the ceiling. It makes no difference in the slightest. They are promptly crushed beneath the tidal wave of undead barreling toward us. They are a wall of rabies-red eyes glowing in the dark, fangs gleaming, claws flashing.

My blood turns to ice, and I push Mrs. Colding on.

Ahead, there's a faint rectangle of dark blue: the entrance to the outside.

"You're going to blow it, right?" I pant, my legs on fire.

"Is that a joke?" Mrs. Colding shouts back.

When we burst out onto the drawbridge, I don't hesitate. Before we've even reached the tender boat bobbing at the end, I jerk up the Glock and pop off three quick rounds, severing the mooring line tied to the bridge's dock cleat in a spit of sparks and puff of torn rope fibers. Then we're diving into the boat, crashing over the cushions into the bottom, and Mrs. Colding is up and tossing the detonator to me and grabbing the helm, frantically turning the engine on, backing the tender away as the army of Volok's worshippers boil out of the tunnel and I'm picking them off with the Glock. One jumps onto the bow and I put a bullet through its forehead, blasting it off into the water and leaving a red smear on the wood paneling. "Faster!" I shout over my shoulder, and Mrs. Colding revs the engine.

When I turn back, another vamp is arcing through the air onto the boat, tackling me.

We crash into the cushions on the starboard side and the detonator goes flying, landing on the bow. The breath goes out of me in whuff, and I push that thing off me and lunge for the detonator. A sudden grip on my leg and I'm hauled away from it, flopping into the floor of the boat. I twist away and kick out, a frantic terror filling my chest, but that thing is on top of me and I manage to brace a forearm against its throat, keep its snapping fangs inches from my neck, its fetid breath spraying droplets of spit onto my cheeks.

"Redfearn!" Mrs. Colding screams, and wrenches the boat to the side.

It changes everything. I hear the detonator slide dangerously toward the edge of the bow, and the force throws the vamp to the left. It gives me just enough time to muscle the barrel of the gun up, straining against that thing's temple, and clip off the final round.

The bullet exits the other side of the thing's head in a fountain of gore, jerking it away from me.

I spring up, dive toward the detonator just as it slides off the bow—

And catch it, depressing the button on it with a *beep*.

We feel it more than hear it: a rumbling cannonade of almost instantaneous booms deep beneath our feet. The dark green waves light up with clouds of flame far below. Then the glowing clouds are expanding, rushing upward, boiling out of the bubbling water in hissing clouds of steam, turning the dark reflective surfaces of the castle gold. The sea is being scalded.

Then Castle Volok explodes.

Fire rushes out of the tunnel in a gout of ferocious orange, incinerating the last of the vampires on the drawbridge, their wails piercing the night. Windows explode outward in a glittering blizzard of pulverized glass and cooked air. I can feel the heat on my cheeks, my eyebrows singeing, smell the ash of the undead sweeping through the hot wind.

Then the fortress is leaning drunkenly, its shattered pylons crumpling like steel straws, giving way beneath all that monstrous weight in a ponderous groan of metal, and Castle Volok begins to sink slowly into the waves in a catastrophic demise of burning seawater.

Mrs. Colding and I gape.

My mouth is still hanging when I turn to her, dazed and breathless. "You do like a little chaos and destruction."

Her lips pert in that way of hers. Her face is shining, burnished a reddish, golden hue in that infernal light, a sheen of sweat on her brow. One or two flyaway hairs have escaped from her bun.

She shrugs a casual shoulder. "I'm getting used to it."

I round the helm station, holding onto steel struts to keep my footing in the rough chop, so I'm standing next to her. She looks up at me, her face glowing, uncertain, and I take her in. The necklace I gave her. Her black wetsuit. The detonator still in her hand. And it dawns on me now: everything she must have done to pull this off. Obtaining all this black-market equipment. Getting here. Diving into the darkness below that fucking castle to place the charges on those pylons. Overcoming her trauma to brave entering that place with all its horrors.

All for me.

I lift her chin with the crook of my finger. "That was the sexiest fucking thing I've ever seen."

It never gets old—the flush of pleasure I get when I see her blush.

"You were worth it," she smirks, gripping my shirt and pulling me close. She toys with her necklace. "But if you ever leave me like that again, I will kill you myself. Understood?"

I hiccup a laugh and nod, sliding my arms around her, holding her body against mine. "Roger that."

She smiles, her whole face lighting up with it, and I feel as if I could fall into those eyes.

I feel as if I'm home.

"Penelope . . .?" I ask.

"Safe," she says. "Back at the hotel. We can probably still make it back before she wakes."

"So it's done, then," I say, and it hits me now, sucking the air out of my lungs, leaving me feeling hollow and stunned. "We did it. It's over."

"Yes." She's closer now, staring up into my eyes, a thing of heart-stopping beauty in that spark-filled night. "We can leave it all behind us now. We can start fresh. Start a new life. Together."

My throat closes against me. I lift a hand, brush her cheek with the backs of my fingers, and she tilts her head into it and hoods her eyes, lost in that touch.

Then she stiffens all over, eyes flying open as if she's just been zapped by a stripped copper wire, and I feel a cool, dry sensation at the nape of my neck, all the little hairs there standing on end.

She's seen something.

She's looking over my shoulder, and whatever it is has made her nose thin, a muscle twitch at the corner of one eye.

And I see, in those eyes, what she's seeing, reflected in the flame-filled wells of her irises.

I slowly turn, goose bumps prickling down my back.

Castle Volok is almost gone now. As the horns of its spires slip into the waves, something can be seen beyond that veil of burning destruction. A shimmering mirage, a spine-tingling hallucination born of fire, wavery and demonic in the blurry waves of heat: a superyacht made in the high-sterned, round-bellied mode of a Chinese junk. As its prow parts the dancing flames, gliding through like a vengeful phoenix unleashed, I see its carbon fibre mast is being raised in eerie automation, its yardarms falling outwards, unfurling jagged red sails like the leathery folds of dragon wings, a sight of dreadful wonder.

The Steward's ship.

It must be. Released, just in time, from the bowels of the castle before the explosion.

And he's there, standing at the prow. The Steward. I can tell from the robe he's wearing, whipping in the wind. That robe with its shimmery-scaled dragons, spiky heads plunging in wrathful power. They are on the hunt, those dragons, just like their owner. Ready to pursue us to the ends of the earth.

But Mrs. Colding is calling him—calling the Steward—by another name.

"It can't be," she murmurs, voice hushed with terror, and I turn to see her lower a pair of binoculars, their lenses reflecting twin worlds crazed with flames and dragon wings and that slick pale fucker in unwanted duplicate.

"What?" I ask, but I already know. I know by her face, with stomach-twisting certainty, that I won't like what she says next.

"It's him," she states, transfixed, helpless as prey, her eyes unable to tear themselves away from that apparition.

"Who?" I growl, taking her by the shoulders, finally snapping her eyes away.

And she looks into my face.

"It's my ex-husband," she breathes. "It's Mr. Colding."

ABOUT THE AUTHOR

D.V. Sullivan has been a deckhand in the Mediterranean, a bartender in New York and an English teacher in China. Now that he's no longer hosing salt off yachts during high-wind gales, he writes from his lair in the Pacific Northwest.

DVSullivan.com
Facebook.com/AuthorDVSullivan
TikTok @dvsullivanauthor
Instagram @authordavidsullivan
X/Twitter @bydvsullivan